# THE
# ROAD
# TO
# EIN
# HAROD

*Amos Kenan*

# THE
# ROAD
# TO
# EIN
# HAROD

*Translated from the French by Anselm Hollo*

GROVE PRESS
NEW YORK

Copyright © 1984 by Amos Kenan
Translation copyright © 1988 by Anselm Hollo

Originally published in Hebrew
as הדרך לעין חרוד by Am Oved Publishers Ltd,
Tel Aviv, 1984.

Published by Grove Press
a division of Wheatland Corporation
920 Broadway
New York, N.Y. 10010

LIBRARY OF CONGRESS CATALOGING-IN-PUBLICATION DATA

Kenan, Amos, 1927–
The road to Ein Harod.

Originally published in Hebrew under title: ha-Derekh
le-Ein Harod.
I. Title.
PJ5054.K355D4713   1988      892.4'36      86-45249
ISBN 0-8021-1083-5

Designed by Helen Barrow
Manufactured in the United States of America
First Edition 1988
10  9  8  7  6  5  4  3  2  1

# THE
# ROAD
# TO
# EIN
# HAROD

I have been thinking about that pretty song, "The road to the kvutza's* neither short nor long." Actually, Ein Harod is not a kvutza: it used to be an entire kibbutz, and now, after the secession, it is two whole kibbutzim. According to my calculations, with any luck I would be able to get to Ein Harod in three days, a week at the most.

I know that if I want to get to Ein Harod alive, it is quite out of the question to try the road or the train, or even to be seen anywhere near any kind of highway. But that isn't my problem at the moment. Right now, my problem is how to get out of Tel Aviv.

There's only one way: by sea. The land routes are impossible. First of all, there are roadblocks at all the city exits. No way around those. They don't just detain you. In the first two weeks they shot on sight anyone they suspected, rightly or wrongly, of intending to go to Ein Harod. Even those who thought that if they traveled with their families they'd give the impression of heading north quite innocently—even they were mowed down without mercy, children and all.

These days, not even loyalists venture out in their cars by

*For this and other terms and names, see Notes, p. 107.

themselves; the roads are traveled only by organized, controlled, and escorted convoys.

It would be useless to try to get out of Tel Aviv on the back roads, even alone. Patrols are checking every rock pile, every clump of trees, every orchard. Helicopters open fire at the least suspicious movement. Even after dark, in the light of flares slowly descending from airplanes, anyone risking his life to get through is machine-gun fodder.

So the only way out is the sea. Even that has its problems. For one thing, the coast is patrolled day and night. And even if you know the best spot to dive in, you still have to reach that spot alive. Third, there's the question of equipment. You can't hit that road "neither short nor long" without arms, ammunition, and food. Even if you are a good underwater swimmer, a professional frogman or a scuba diver, you still have to tow that stuff along in a watertight container that's easily spotted. The water, too, is well guarded. Patrol boats with rocket launchers cruise it, helicopters and low-flying planes scan its surface, inflatable canoes without lights slide here and there, equipped with sophisticated devices for detecting fugitives. Then there's the final problem: where to get out of the water and start walking.

After careful consideration of all these factors I have decided that I can risk it after all and get going.

Certainly not without counting on luck. Luck had it that my family wasn't at home.

It all started at Hanukkah. I remember that evening. My wife had gone to eat latkes at a friend's house, I had stayed home to get some work done, and the children were camping in the woods of Ben-Shemen. From listening to the radio I know that the children are alive. Only the counselors were killed. The children were detained, and as far as I can tell, in conditions that aren't too awful.

I have a friend in the Old Town of Jaffa. I've decided to go to him. Well, not exactly a friend, but I don't think he'll turn me in. I'm also pretty sure that my wife's friends aren't

going to betray her either. Not that they aren't loyalists—
they are, as far as their ideas go—but they are members of a
dubious profession, and that is why, I assume, they had no
warning as to what was going to happen.

As for the Old Town of Jaffa, we know that it is now mainly
inhabited by artists and the like. But they are the kind of
artists who did not hesitate to take over the houses in which
the old citizens of Jaffa had been living, the ones who had to
flee by sea in 1948. Anyone capable of living in the house of
someone forced to become a refugee won't be a traitor, you
can count on it. Unfortunately, I have to count on their
loyalty to me as well.

It was by pure chance that I found out about it all. There
was nothing on the radio, on TV, in the newspapers. I don't
know what made me start playing with the radio dial that
evening. I was looking for a foreign station. And then I
heard a voice that said, in Hebrew, "This is Free Ein Harod.
Attention, this is Free Ein Harod calling." At first I thought
it was some kind of hoax. There are enough crazies who have
their own transmitters. But the story they were telling
wasn't funny. I turned the TV on; the announcer was read-
ing the news in his habitual fashion, and there was nothing
remarkable in it. I called my wife's friends. She picked up
the phone, sounding happy, and in the background I heard
the friends' children singing "Day of Hanukkah, Inaugura-
tion of Our Temple." I felt reassured.

Around eleven o'clock that night the doorbell rang. I asked
who it was, and the voice of my neighbor's daughter replied
that it was my neighbor.

For some time now I have not opened the door without
holding in my hand, at the ready, a little tear gas canister I
picked up in New York. I also carry a knife in my pocket at
all times. As soon as I opened the door I knew something
was wrong and sprayed the tear gas at two men who had
been standing on either side of the door so as not to be seen
through the peephole. One of them managed to pull a

revolver, so I killed him on the spot. The other one fainted. So did the neighbor's girl.

I did some fast thinking. I took the unconscious man's gun and pulled him inside. Then I dragged in the neighbor's daughter, and finally the dead man. I took his gun too.

I tied the live ones' wrists and ankles with lengths of clothesline and gagged them by stuffing rags in their mouths and taping them down, just like in the movies. Then I sat down in the armchair and vomited. I started shaking all over, violently, hysterically. Then came tears and hiccups. I grabbed a bottle of whiskey and didn't bother with a glass.

I did some furious thinking.

The contractor who built this house didn't do too good a job. I have always hated the attics. They are very long and narrow, like tunnels, so that it is impossible to make use of their entire length. There is no way to store a suitcase at the far end unless you crawl on your belly like an Indian on the warpath through rubble and bits of wire, pushing the suitcase ahead of you. God bless that contractor.

At top speed I gathered up all the canned goods in the house and filled a few containers with water. Took the Walkman with its earphones. A flashlight. Batteries. The guns. My military uniform—it might come in handy.

Then I went through all the rooms and emptied drawers and wardrobes quickly, like someone who has to pack in a panic. I even thought about the piss and shit question: it was absolutely necessary to prevent bad odors from escaping. Who knew how long I would have to stay up there, flat on my stomach? I thought of the prophet Ezekiel, who spent a year and some months lying on one side, and a few more months on the other, and who all that time ate barley cakes baked in his own shit. I'm no prophet, so I don't have to eat shit. Had I been one, I would have done so already, before all this trouble started. Now there's no point in it.

Worrying about the odor, I carried up a few large empty

cans and all the detergents I found under the sink. I had read somewhere that the main effect of all those detergents and deodorizers was to anesthetize the user's sense of smell. I decided to believe it.

I went to the front door and opened it wide. I climbed up into the attic and closed its door behind me.

I gave myself two weeks. They'll find the front door open. They'll come in and stumble over a dead body and two tied-up prisoners. It will be better still if those prisoners manage to free themselves and go for help. No one will think of looking for me in an apartment where I have killed a man. Even if they search the place, no one will start crawling through the attic on his stomach.

Not that every good and true calculation always turns out to be correct. But what choice do I have? If they kill me, they kill me. At least I'll get a few of them first. I have never kept firearms in the house. People who favor quick decisions shouldn't have firearms handy. Someone who might suddenly feel like committing suicide is better off without immediate access to such an elegant, easy, quick, and painless tool. Better for him if he finds it inconvenient to carry out what might be a whim instantly. But here I am, with my guns.

They came three-quarters of an hour later. They fired long bursts. Into all the rooms. They even fired into the attic. Had there been an architect among them, they would have noticed that there was something strange about this long corridor with its low ceiling leading from the entrance to the living room. Why would it be so low, the whole way, when the opening from the kitchen to the attic is so narrow? But apparently none of them was an architect.

They stopped shooting and proceeded to break things. To shout. Then they asked for instructions over their walkie-talkie. I heard them mention an ambulance. Then they left, slamming the front door. I know that sound.

I didn't even think of coming out.

So now I have been here for two weeks. Today's the day I intend to leave.

The first few days, the door would open from time to time. People came and went, stole whatever they could. I knew pretty much what they were taking because they discussed the division of the loot in loud voices. Then, for a few days, some kind of headquarters or liaison office was set up in the apartment. People arrived and left, the telephone rang constantly, the radios were working full time. Once or twice, at night, the men guarding the place made love to their girl-friends. I heard it all. The neighbor's daughter too.

All along I was listening to Radio Ein Harod on my Walk-man. I got the whole story, piecing it together. They said that the entire region was under their control and that they had so far been able to repulse all attacks, including aerial ones. I have no idea how much of this is true and how much is just designed to boost morale.

Perhaps—who knows?—there is only this one solitary broadcaster left, dreaming out loud. In some kind of final bunker that hasn't been shelled to pieces yet. I also heard their warnings not to try to join them by ordinary means.

So there must be others like me. But where does Radio Ein Harod get its news? The news is being relayed to them continuously, from all over. Perhaps there is some kind of clandestine organization. Perhaps some people foresaw what was about to happen and established cells of supporters and an emergency communications network. On the other hand, no one got in touch with me. I'm not complaining. True, I've never made a secret of my views. Perhaps my time is over. I'm not complaining about that either. You can't dictate to people, not even to your friends, what place they should assign you.

The most disconcerting thing is that there's not a word about Ein Harod on the official radio. I listen to all the official communiqués. Orders to obey. Orders to obey orders. Orders banning all gatherings. And orders not to travel anywhere without approved permits. Nothing about Ein Harod. Is that because it no longer exists?

But I have no choice. I have to go there. If Ein Harod exists, it is my place.

Will I be allowed to see my loved ones again one day?

Now it has been four days since the door to the apartment last opened. Silence reigns. I'm leaving tonight.

Certainly not by the elevator. Nor by the stairs. It is the thieves' hour.

By means of a rope, through the window, like a thief. And here I am in the courtyard.

I've changed my plan. It will be impossible to get to Jaffa by land. The vast wasteland between Tel Aviv and Jaffa would be a trap. I'll have to take the risk and get to the sea in Tel Aviv itself, as close to my house as possible.

A jump, from my yard into the next. Then across the street, just like in the old days. Then through other yards and into the next street. And here's the promenade. White waves. A dark sea.

Now or never. It's the thieves' hour. No moon. It is drizzling. Dear old friend, nocturnal rain. A friend from other nights in the past. I'm in the water. Nothing has happened. No one has shot at me, no one has caught me in a cone of light. No one has shouted, "Who goes there?" I'm in good shape. Others have managed to escape from places sealed off tighter than Tel Aviv.

I'm planning to swim as far as Sidna Ali. A godforsaken place. One mosque with the tomb of a saint on a tiny cape jutting out into the sea. These small capes on the coast of Eretz Israel are where the enemy has always surged out of the water to conquer the land, and where he has fled on the last boat when the land snapped shut on him. And here I am, fleeing from my country toward my country.

There used to be an Arab village there, forgotten now, and a radar station, still there, and a transit camp for new immigrants, abandoned long ago but still there. This was the Reshef of the Canaanites, the Apollonia of the Greeks, and Ali Ben-Guleim fell and was buried here in 1081, and it was here that Richard Coeur de Lion defeated Saladin for the last time in 1191 until Baybars came in 1265 and drove the Crusaders out, and here the British fought the Turks in 1917 and drove them from the coastal plain. A place forgotten within the boundaries of Herzlia the Glorious, not far from Tel Aviv the Crowned. And it is where I have to be, before the sun rises. I can do it in three and a half hours. Once upon a time, it would have been child's play. Now, frankly, it will be harder. But when there's no choice, there's no choice.

I swim along in the dark, and something makes me laugh. According to my original plan, I would have gone to Jaffa. My so-called friend's house is built into the city wall. Like Rahab, the harlot of Jericho. Rest in peace, harlot of Jaffa, no spy will come to your house tonight.

I don't know why I am singing a Ukrainian song to myself, one my grandmother used to sing to me. The story of a peasant. I once saw her combing her hair, and it reached down all the way to her knees.

I recite the list of students in my Aleph class. Alfandari Amir Begelman Berez Berlanczyk Ben-Aharon Grinschpon Gabaï Dichter Ditkowski Dagan Horn Warschawsky Venarsky Sonschein Zeitman Sussman Taxin Yudelewitch Kaspi Levin Lifschitz Landau Daniel Landau Ygal Lehrman Miller Mizrahi Maroschek Salomon Segalowitch Fucksman Perleman Polaniewsztsky Zeelengold Zimmerman Sipor Kreiner Kachtan Shalit Schönfarber Schmerling Schlang.

At night, you swim without fear. At night, the sea embraces you. In the daytime, when I swam long distances, I used to be afraid of monsters that would rise from the depths of the sea.

Once or twice I've heard an airplane. No patrol boats, no helicopters, none of the frightening things they've been threatening us with. Perhaps they have devoted two weeks to spreading terror and the operation is over now.

I get there before dawn, naked and shivering. My clothes and all my gear in a watertight bag. The rest of the way I have to crawl.

Here, sandstone hills stretch right down to the sea. Erosion has formed small creeks. What I need is a ravine.

For several reasons. First of all, it would provide cover. But more important, it's only by following a ravine that I'll be able to clear the most difficult obstacle, the coastal highway.

Naked, I scramble up the steep ravine to a level spot. From here, I'll have to trust in luck. Because this is where the coastal plain begins, quite abruptly. I have to take care not to get too close to Herzlia. I have to stay in no-man's-land.

Although I am wearing light rubber swimming shoes, I find it hard to walk over the thorns and sharp-edged rocks. It's time for me to put on my clothes, to look like a human being.

Time is my adversary now. My trembling fingers struggle with the shoelaces. I don't know whether I'm shivering with fear or cold or both, and shit, it's daybreak already.

There are two coastal roads. One, close to the shore, is the hotel road. The other, farther east, is the highway.

How many times have I crawled like this? Each time you think it'll be the last. Because this is the time you're going to get killed. Or because this will be the last war. But when I crawled before, it was to emerge from the depths of the night and fall upon an enemy who wasn't expecting me in that place or at that hour. This time I'm on the run.

I have to find the aqueduct that passes under the road, but the lay of the terrain makes it difficult. On this plain, it's hard to figure out where it'll be. Nevertheless, it's the only way I can get past the road, and also the only place to hide.

I almost fall onto a tank dug in between the coastal road and the cliff. I should have known. They weren't born yesterday either. What saves me is the smell of a cigarette. There is no sign of a glowing tip. The fellow on guard remembers his training. Glued to the ground, I strain my eyes and see the outline of the tank. Then I see that there are three of them. Only their turrets and guns stick out of the trench. With great care and for what seems like an eternity I crawl backward until I know I'm below the horizon they're scanning.

Now I understand why the tanks are here. There's the little bridge in the road, and the aqueduct below it. A spot for lovers, a spot for rapists, a place for vagabonds to take a shit, for brigands to share their loot, for saboteurs to plant a bomb under the bridge and blow up the road, and I should have known—oh, yes, I certainly should have known.

A nearsighted fugitive is quite a joke. Except for the cigarette, there's no doubt who would have seen who first.

This is no time to hesitate. Very soon the crew is going to wake up, and I'll be a goner. I crawl forward, knowing that I may be discovered at any moment. I reach the aqueduct, pass under the bridge, and now I am on the other side. From here, walking fast and crouching low, I make it to the main highway and under it.

Beyond the highway lies the beautiful old kingdom of Sharon's orange groves. From here, from the orchards of Sharon, we once surged forth to conquer Vaheb by storm.

The road to the kvutza, I say and repeat, is neither short nor long.

Except that this time, unlike all the other times, it has a different aspect.

Not like in the beautiful days or nights. Nor in memories. Not in what used to be. And not in what you used to be. Nor in what you want to be or dream of being.

What you have been is dead. What you wanted is dead.

Memory, too, is dead. Only you are alive, only you are still alive, echo and memory, shadow and reflection, end of days whose beginning has been lost along the road that is neither short nor long.

I have to find an Arab. Without the help of an Arab I'll never reach Wadi Ara. My entire escape plan is based on Arabs.

For me, the most dangerous area is the region of Sharon, that gigantic coastal town that extends from Tel Aviv to the north and never really ends. If I want to get to Ein Harod, I have to cross Sharon eastward and get to the hills of the Arab Triangle. From there, past Wadi Ara to Megiddo. The question is where to find Arabs and what has happened to them in all this turmoil. And to think that it was I who drove the Arabs out of here. I, with Shaltiel and David and all the others—we drove them out and conquered Vaheb by storm. Some other time I would have rolled on the ground with laughter at the irony. But now isn't that time, and the irony doesn't make me laugh. What wouldn't I give now to run into Ahmed, Mahmoud, Hassan, or Ali and tell them, Take me along, help me to get out of here.

I would arrive in the village. Fatima would go down to the well to fetch water for the sheep and the goats, and I would roll the stone off the well for her. But there is no more Fatima, there are no sheep, there is no well, nor is there a stone. No point in putting on an abaya and kafiya to look like an Arab, because it's been a long time since Arabs looked like Arabs. And I wouldn't even know what to do to look like a Jew who looks like an Arab.

Only if I manage to get to the orange groves will I stand a chance. Once, long ago, this was our kingdom, the cradle of the revolution, home of the brave, refuge for those who were destined to conquer all and change everything. Now it's all concrete. But there must still be some orchards. Maybe Shaltiel's orchard is still there. And perhaps in Shaltiel's orchard I'll find Mahmoud. He is waiting for me there, has been waiting since 1948. He's hiding, but I know how to find him because I, like him, come from orchards.

A wasteland stretches out in front of me. Thorn bushes. Piles of rubble, old tires, empty barrels, heaps of tin cans. A white trail among the thorns, with a residential development at the end of it.

A kid comes out with a huge dog. Hour of the dogs. Then it'll be the hour of breakfast, the morning news, then time to start the car, go to work, to school.

Here I won't find an Arab. Here I have to look for a woman.

I need to examine everything very carefully. Knowing how myopic I am, I have brought a pair of binoculars. Now I have to watch the courtyards. See the wife come out with her husband and kid, walk them to the car. Scrutinize her face, make some conjectures, draw some conclusions. And hope for luck. That woman whose face I have examined, who has been the subject of my conjectures and conclusions, will then have to wave to the car and go back into her house. What I need, however, is a woman who has a second car. A woman without a car wouldn't be any use to me. I have thought about all this, about all these things, down to the tiniest detail, back there in my attic lying on my side in urine and shit. From the woman onward the road is neither short nor long.

In the wasteland I have found a kind of scout's tent made out of two metal sheets propped against each other, a windbreak for the construction workers who built this place. From here, there's an excellent view of the first row of houses. I wait. No one comes out before seven-thirty. I light a cigarette. Up to this day, of all the enemies I wanted to kill, I have managed to kill only time without difficulty.

Now they're beginning to start up their cars, that morning symphony of respectable folk.

I think about them without bitterness or contempt. I have

no more thoughts on the subject of respectable folk. All that is over. Now I have time only for dreams.

A tall man, good-looking, puts his two children in the back seat; his wife gets in beside him. One less to consider. I look at her and ask myself what I would have done if she had stayed at home. No.

One by one they go to their tasks. Fat, skinny, bald and potbellied, tall, short, with sons and daughters, cute and not so cute, with more or less beautiful and well-groomed wives or not so beautiful and well-groomed ones, more or less.

In all the rows of houses, only two women have stayed home. Which one?

Take it easy. Maybe one of the husbands has forgotten something. Give them time to make a few phone calls and take care of morning routines. No point in going in before they have settled in an armchair with a book or a newspaper or something. Which one of the two?

One has a small Fiat, the other a sports car. Women always have the smaller cars.

The one with the Fiat is about thirty, thirty-five. Slim, fragile, wears glasses. The one with the sports car is taller, elegant, closer to forty. The one with the Fiat might understand better, accept more. The one with the convertible might not even want to know what it was about but might be bored enough to go for an adventure. To be sure, I have to anticipate the case in which the woman does not want to help me, either out of fear or hostility. She might even try to turn me in if she can. That would be the time for the revolver.

Tough decision. The less indifferent one might be willing to help but might not know how. She might panic in an unexpected situation. As for the one with the convertible, I can't count on anything at all in her case, but I know that nothing can panic her. So I pick the convertible.

I ring the doorbell.

She opens the door at the first ring. Must have heard my footsteps.

Brief scrutiny.

Come in.

I come in.

I don't like to talk to people on the doorstep. Now tell me what you want.

I want help.

That's what I thought. Who are you?

My name won't mean anything to you.

I don't see how I can help you.

You have a car.

I have an ass too.

Right now I'm not interested in ass.

I didn't think you came here for that. Then again, why not?

My kingdom for a horse, I say.

You don't look to me like you have a kingdom.

I wouldn't say no to a cup of coffee.

Coffee, sure. But why should I help you?

Because I have no choice.

You're one of those.

Yes, I'm one of those.

I'm not.

What are you one of?

One of those who have. Don't stand there. Have a seat. I'll make some coffee.

I sit down. From the kitchen I hear those sounds that used to be ordinary. I look at the walls. Paintings. Books. Stereo. Television. All the ordinary things. Several paintings signed by artists I had known well. I wonder what has become of them. Some of them knew which side their bread was buttered on. And others didn't. Then there were those who couldn't make up their minds fast enough. And there's always the one who commits suicide. I wonder which one of them has, and whether it was for a good reason.

Once, years ago, at five o'clock in the morning in a bistro, one of them asked me if that was what I would advise him to do. I told him it was. Ah, those were the days. That was his last attempt to become my friend.

An agreeable aroma of good coffee wafts in from the kitchen. My knees turn to water and I start shaking. What the world used to be and will never be again.

When she brings the coffee she gives me a curious look. I know she has noticed.

Listen, why don't you just turn yourself in? she says. Wouldn't that be easier?

I've told you that I'm one of those who have no choice.

You're on the list.

Yes, I'm on the list.

I should have guessed. I wasn't sure.

But now you are.

Yes, but it's not good. Drink your coffee, you need it now. Be quiet, don't say anything.

I keep quiet. The coffee is strong and good. The world is dead only for the dead, and I'm still alive.

I've stopped shaking now. I have been thinking about the man who might or might not have killed himself, and if he did, then as usual it was for no good reason.

Well, you seem to have cheered up all of a sudden, she says. Like God when an angel sucks him off.

There's no God, I tell her, and no angel either.

I could try it anyway.

I burst out laughing. Here I am, a fugitive whose life hangs by a thread, as good as dead, and here comes this last grace, and if that isn't funny, I don't know what is. But think of it—as long as you can laugh you have your whole life ahead of you, and that's another reason to laugh.

I wasn't born yesterday, and all kinds of things have happened to me. But all of a sudden I forget that I'm a fugitive, and I know only one thing: I want her to.

She has been looking at me without smiling.

I know that look. It's the one a runaway gives to a fugitive.

I'll get some cognac and give you a dash of it in your coffee, and you'll tell me what you need.

The cognac gets to me, and for an instant the world is the way it was or the way it should be.

I have to get to an Arab village. Tira, Taibeh, Kalansawa—it doesn't matter which one.

But that's impossible. You know, don't you, that they've been surrounded and there's a curfew.

I didn't know that. Just take me close, and I'll continue on foot.

Why don't you listen to some music. I'll be ready in five minutes. No use waiting until it gets dark, because then they won't ask questions, they'll just shoot. And I have an appointment with my hairdresser at noon.

She puts on a record and leaves the room. It's a little piece by Mozart for violin and piano that I haven't heard before.

She comes back wearing tight pants, says that she's ready, and laughs. Why are you laughing? I ask her, and she tells me it's because of those pants.

I know why she's laughing. If there's anything in the world really stripped and naked, it's not an ass with its dress pulled up but an ass with its pants pulled down.

A cloud in trousers has come to offer a nonexistent kingdom for a filly in tight pants.

We go out, get into the car.

Her hair, as they say in poems, floats in the wind, she steps on the gas, and I don't want to look at the speedometer but can tell that we're really making tracks.

Fields, orchards rush by, the air is full of fragrances, and we are approaching the hills in the east on our way to the road to freedom.

She slows down gently, turns onto a little dirt road between orange groves, stops, turns the engine off.

There isn't a sound to be heard. There is no breeze, and her hair is no longer blowing in the wind but rests peacefully on her head. I figure that we are two or three kilometers from the village. At night it will be child's play to cross the lines and get there. And then . . . Allah akbar.

She looks at me, smiling, and unzips my trousers in one swift gesture.

It is one of those moments when a man gives up his soul to his Maker or returns to his mother's womb or something of that sort. Not that I agree with her fable about God and his angel. But here we are, and that's that.

It must have been a stray bullet, otherwise I couldn't have rolled out of the car alive.

Suddenly she is dead, and I feel and then see her head snap back and my sperm flow across her face, her eyelids, her eyes.

I am not dead. Her eyes glaze over and I jump out of the car. There's no time for questions—what is an enemy dead at your feet and what is a friend dead at your feet when you are facing death with an open fly?

I disappear into the orange grove to wait until dark and then try to reach the village. In the end, I never got to see her ass. She was right to laugh about that. More's the pity.

What was her name? Oh, hell. Probably in her purse. I once had a friend who used to say, All this is very nice now, but what about tonight? And that's all I want to know now too.

It won't be night for a while. It's going to be a long day. From here on in, he who wants to see must not be seen, and he who wants to hear must not be heard. I make myself as small as possible, but it is hard to really hide in an orange grove. Anyone who decides to enter the grove and look for you is going to find you.

God's own silence. Not a fly, not a bird, not a distant car, not a human voice. Why this silence? Am I alone now?

My batteries are dead, I've lost touch with the outside world. What has become of Ein Harod? Where are they all?

I'm no longer alone. There's a helicopter in the sky. Distant, weak at first, but I can tell. A white sports car and a dead woman. A quick radio message. Then they'll come in their armored cars. One, two, three and more, as many as they need. The helicopter comes closer, becomes a roll of thunder. Slowly and lazily it turns above me. Is this the site of my grave?

They'll bring trackers, no doubt. A good tracker is worse than a dog. Now I hear another helicopter. They probably took off together, and now the one above me has put out a call. If I had a last cigarette this would be the right moment, but I've already smoked my last one back in the wasteland. They'll probably bring dogs too.

If she had turned south on the road, I wouldn't have stood a chance. But she headed north, and I won't have to cross any east-west road between here and Natania. I have to keep moving north and east, and fast. No time to waste crawling and hiding. Nothing for it but to run like a demon, pursued by all the demons, with nothing to lose.

I run and I fall, I get up and I run, I fall, I get up, I run. I am still in the orange grove, and in spite of everything there's still a chance they haven't spotted me. If they have, I'll find out all right. I take care not to stray from the line of trees, I run only on that very line. The branches of the trees touch one another, each row is a continuous and dense mass, perhaps they won't see me. But what'll happen at the end of the grove?

Maybe I shouldn't run. How long can a man keep running anyway? Maybe I should stop and wait for them. Or kill myself. Or take one or two of them with me before the hail of bullets cuts me down. Or raise my hands, surrender.

I'm at the edge of the orchard. There's a barricade. It's the moment to wake up in terror, covered in cold sweat, and realize it was a dream.

To wake up where? In my attic, in the shit, knowing that all this horror hasn't begun yet? Or to wake up even earlier, a month ago, a year ago, and know that everything that's happened since has been just a dream?

Or perhaps wake up two years ago. Or ten years ago. Or perhaps not wake up at all, perhaps go on running through the horror, toward a greater horror, endlessly.

Here's the edge of the orchard, here's the place, here's the moment to decide what's next. I take out my revolver.

A revolver is an urban weapon, and not very reliable at that. A revolver is a weapon with which you can kill someone you're out to get, not someone who's out to get you.

Beyond the orchard there's a dirt road, beyond that road another orchard. No use looking for a wadi here. Where there's a wadi there are hills, and where there are hills there are no orchards. Instead there are vineyards and olive groves, and that's a different story altogether, and suddenly I am stuck in that goddamn verse from the Book of Psalms, Thy wife is a fertile vine in the outermost reach of thy house, thy sons olive seedlings around thy table, and I am here, but where is my vine, where are my seedlings, and where am I?

I lie down on the ground. I think things over. Suddenly someone bounds out of the opposite orchard, crosses the sandy road, and almost lands on top of me.

Mahmoud.

At first he doesn't see me. But he is alert. Flat on his stomach, he scans the terrain, and then comes the inevitable moment when our eyes meet.

He is about thirty years younger than me. Well built. But I don't see a weapon on him, and I have a revolver. This is his first warpath, but it is my last.

He has seen the gun pointed at him. We are both flat on the ground, and both of us have to make a very quick decision. I understand that it is hard for him to figure out whether I'm not shooting at him because I'm afraid of the noise or because I have no intention of shooting at him. I decide to decide first.

Shalom, I say.

He doesn't reply. He looks at me. I wait, then say it again: Shalom.

You don't say shalom with a revolver.

I'm for peace with security, and what's your name?

Mahmoud, if that's all right with you. And you won't have that peace.

Where are you from?

Tira.

What are you doing here?

I'm running from the soldiers.

Where to?

I don't know.

Why did you cross over here?

There were soldiers on the other side.

How many?

A lot. Ten. Twenty.

What's east of here?

This orchard. It goes a long way east.

And west?

The sea. Where we'll drive you. All of you.

You're one of those.

Well, what did you think?

I'm not "all of you."

For me, all of you are all of you.

You really hate us.

I've got nothing else to live for.

You'd like to kill me.

I would.

I could kill you.

Do it.

Listen, Mahmoud. If we don't do something together, and fast, they'll kill us both.

Don't talk to me like I'm a peasant. I have been to the university.

So?

So I don't want any favors from you, and I won't do you any favors either. All you can do is force me. With your revolver.

Idiot. Let's get out of here before they kill both of us. Then we'll see who gets to kill who. Now, run ahead of me.

No running.

Then walk.

We start walking. Under the rows of trees, from west to east. Mahmoud is quiet, I am quiet. Not once does he look back, but I keep my distance. Security.

Then I hear armored cars on the road. Not just one or two, a whole convoy of them. It is impossible not to hear them, even with the racket the helicopters are making. They are moving along the road to the south, which is quite close by. Mahmoud goes on walking as if he hasn't heard a thing. Never leaving the cover of the trees so as not to be seen from the dirt road or the highway or from above.

Now I see where he's taking me. To an old packing shed for oranges. These days those sheds aren't used anymore. For some unknown reason this particular one hasn't been torn down.

I follow him inside.

My father used to work in this grove before I was born. For the Jews. Let me show you something.

He walks to a corner, brings back a rubber plunger. He sticks it onto a large floor tile and pulls.

Look. Do you know what this is? This is where you hid your weapons in the British days. My father showed me the cache when I was a kid. You called it a *slik*.

Go on down.

You won't know how to close that tile right.

Just go on down, don't worry. I dealt with tiles like this one before you were born.

He goes down ahead of me. I switch on my flashlight. I follow him down and pull the tile shut the way I remember.

Turn off the light. We'll need it when it gets dark.

I'll do that, but only after I tie your hands and feet.

You're not going to tie me up. You can't.

That's what you think. I pull out my tear gas and let him

have it in the face. Surprised and shocked, he cries out and grabs his head with both hands. I hit him on the head with the butt of my gun. He crumples. My eyes are tearing and I'm coughing, but I'm still on my feet. I shine the light on the concrete tunnel. If I can find something to tie him up with, we'll both be better off.

I can't find a thing. No rope, no steel wire, no electric wire, no shoelaces, no old sheets.

Now I can turn off the flashlight. I do, and wait. The darkness isn't total. Perhaps there's a hidden ventilation shaft or something like that. There won't be any problems until nightfall.

Mahmoud wakes up. I can't see his expression.

See, I told you you couldn't tie me up.

Sorry about your head, I say. I had to do it. I had no choice.

We always make you hit us. You never have a choice.

Go to hell, I tell him. You're a pain in the ass.

Neither of us says anything for a while.

D'you have a cigarette? I ask him.

Yes.

Light one for me and roll it over here.

He lights one for himself and one for me and rolls it to me. We remain silent. In the glow of his cigarette I can see blood on his forehead.

You probably think I'm your prisoner.

I don't think anything.

I'd say that you're my prisoner.

You don't say.

Maybe you think I'm afraid of you and your gun.

I told you, I don't think, period.

He smokes in silence. He puts his cigarette out on the concrete floor. I extinguish mine a few seconds later. I can't see his face anymore. Just a silhouette.

There's this Jewish chick in Natania I've been screwing.

I'm not interested in your screwing.

What she likes best is when I stick it up her ass.

I don't comment.

She really loves it up her ass. She just loves it when I shove it in. You hear me?

No.

Stop lying. You hear me all right.

I'm lying. I can't hear you.

She thinks I'm a Jew. She thinks that I'm a Jew and my name is Rafi. In Natania everyone calls me Rafi.

Congratulations.

I'm doing all right.

Let me tell you how you're doing. You're not Mahmoud. You're not Rafi. You're just a piece of shit, and that's all. A stinking piece of shit, that's what you are. If there's one thing in the world that really stinks, it's someone who is not himself and is someone else, because anything that's not itself isn't anything else either. It's just shit, that's all, so get out of my sight, I don't even want to look at such garbage.

I'll kill you right now, by God, I'll kill you.

One move and I'll shoot.

He moves. I pull the trigger. I'm not aiming at him. I fire to one side, at the concrete. The noise is deafening. I am stunned. He is stunned.

Nothing happens. Perhaps no one has heard. After that din, the silence rings in our ears. Suddenly he starts crying.

See what you've done to us, he wails, see what you've done to us. You think I don't know that I'm just shit? You think I'm proud when I shove it up her ass? I feel like someone's shoving it up my ass, that's how I feel.

What do you want me to do, I ask him, you want me to cry? Or you want me to have a sore ass instead of you? I don't have the strength to cry anymore, I can't even feel sore anymore.

But something's still hurting you.

I told you, I'm not hurting. I told you, I just don't have the strength. Do you have another cigarette?

Again he lights one for himself and one for me. But he doesn't roll it to me, he gets up and hands it to me.

I know you won't shoot me. You could have killed me a moment ago. So I owe you one now. Just one. One time when I won't kill you even though I could.

He goes back to his spot. The blood on his forehead has dried. We sit there in silence.

But don't you start believing that I've suddenly discovered we're both human beings.

I don't believe anything.

You're not a human being. Just look at you. Neither am I.

Why, then?

Believe it or not, I don't know.

Listen, I say. I don't know about you, but I've missed a night's sleep. And the night ahead of us is going to be a long one, we'll have a lot to do. I'm going to sleep now, and you'll wake me up when it's night.

Why do you trust me?

Because I'm exhausted. And because I have no choice. And because I don't know why. Now let's not talk anymore. I have to sleep.

I put the revolver on the floor.

I wake up in a blinding glare. The flashlight is pointed directly into my eyes. The revolver is in Mahmoud's hand.

It's night. Time to go.

Give me the gun.

No way. That's the condition: I'm ready to help you, but only if I get to keep the gun.

Why?

Because if you have the gun I'll betray you and both of us will die.

My, you're touchy.

I'm not touchy. I just want to stay alive.

Well, let's pray you'll have something to stay alive for. Amen.

Insh'Allah.

In a way, I couldn't care less who holds on to the gun, and not only because I remember the revolver in my pocket, the other one I took from the men who had come to kill me. I also know that if the revolver in his hand gives him the feeling that he is not acting under duress, we both have a chance of getting out of this.

He keeps the gun yet walks ahead of me. He raises the big floor tile, climbs out, and helps me up. Thirty years between us: quite a difference.

Where to?

Ein Harod.

You're crazy. You don't stand a chance.

With you, maybe.

And what chance do I have with you?

The same I have with you.

All right. Ein Harod is on my way.

Where are you going?

Farther, he says.

We say nothing more.

I'm no novice at night marches, nearsighted or not. But I have never seen anything like this university-educated villager. He walks on the ground the way an eagle soars in the sky.

We hear voices from all directions. He keeps us gliding right between them all, like bats. We walk very quickly. It's a mistake to think that to go quietly you have to go slowly. It's just the other way around. The faster you move, the more surefooted you are. In its exertion, the leg always finds some solid purchase, something that won't crumble, slip, or make a sound to give you away. I figure we cover some thirty kilometers before daybreak.

We get to a stand of eucalyptus trees. At the far end of it there is water of some kind, a stream, swamp, or drainage ditch. In it grows some dense vegetation, reeds, all kinds of bamboo. A sanctuary for wild pigs.

Two big boars appear, calm and proud, out of some

depression or tunnel in the undergrowth. They don't even look at us. Now I know I'm not considered a human being anymore: even the pigs see me as a brother.

We slip into the hole to sleep in the space the pigs have vacated for us.

I wake up first.

There is still daylight at the end of the hole. Mahmoud is asleep, the gun lies on the ground. I take it and put it in my pocket. It means nothing now, if it ever did. I look for my binoculars, find them, and crawl out.

I'm thirsty and hungry. In the distance to my right are the Ephraim Mountains. In front of me are the hills cut by the single pass from Wadi Ara toward Megiddo. Woods border orchards, and there are more woods beyond. I walk down toward what looks like a stream. It's a murky swamp. A foul smell rises from the water. There is an abundance of edible plants, wild celery, watercress. If there was only a source of fresh water, we could pick them, wash them, eat them. But there isn't. The water is evil.

Mahmoud is standing beside me. I didn't hear him approach. He looks at the swamp, makes a face.

You see, you thought you had drained all the swamps, but you didn't know there'd always be one more.

Well, so what? I say. What if there always is one more?

It means that there's always some more of us and that all of you will drown in this swamp one day.

Oh, leave me alone, Mahmoud.

I can't, says Mahmoud. You have the gun.

He doesn't even crack a smile. Go figure it out.

The sun begins to set behind a distant row of cypresses. From here you can hear the traffic on the coastal highway. There it is, a silver ribbon in the evening light. Military convoys are rolling along, but buses too, undoubtedly checked and authorized to travel north.

My ears pick up another sound, closer by. Mahmoud also hears it and shudders briefly. Two armored personnel carriers drive up to the woods. Come to a halt. The side doors of one of them open and some people are pushed out, blindfolded, their hands tied behind their backs. A group of armed soldiers piles out of the second vehicle.

The people with the blindfolds and tied hands seem to be of all ages. Some are women. I recognize one of the men. It is the painter whose suicide I have fantasized about. Here he is. Has he been trying to reach Ein Harod despite everything and been caught on the way? Yes, most likely. If he had been picked up in Tel Aviv, there would have been no need to drag him all the way out here. What a small country, I say to myself, the places you get to see. One of the military men, an officer it seems, orders the others to line up. He takes out a piece of paper and reads something out loud. Then he stands aside. A brief order. Fire. The people fall down. A small bulldozer drives up and quickly digs a ditch. The soldiers roll the bodies in, and the dozer covers them up with a big mound of earth.

The vehicles return the way they came, the landscape has swallowed everything, rain will erase the tracks, and the earth is used to these things.

So, we can go on now. I look for a smirk on Mahmoud's face. Had it been there, I would have wiped it out with my fists. It wasn't.

I haven't asked you your name yet, he says.

You can call me Rafi.

Now Mahmoud smiles. Let's get a move on, he says. We head eastward.

His reckoning is right. If we want to go by way of Wadi Ara, we have to climb its right shoulder, on the east. There are no roads there, nothing but stony hills, olive groves, fallow land, oak and pine woods.

I follow in Mahmoud's footsteps, but not blindly. I have ears too, and I know the region quite well. I also have to watch out, because it is possible that he's leading me into a trap. Once in that trap, we would owe each other nothing.

What are the children doing right now? And my wife, where can she be hiding—if they haven't carted her off already? Better, perhaps, if she gave herself up: maybe they'd let her be with the children.

I have to get to Megiddo. Megiddo, I know it well. It is the place they call Armageddon.

There, at Armageddon, the last terrible war is going to be fought, the war of annihilation. To reach Ein Harod I have to pass through Megiddo. There is no other way. There never has been any other way.

Ever since Ramses, this is where the die has been cast. Since Ramses, the battle of Megiddo has been the decisive one, and since Ramses, brother, Armageddon has been waiting for you.

Another quick march. No moonlight. Not one pebble rolls, not one dry twig cracks, and the air is filled with a powerful smell, the smell of damp soil and small juicy plants mashed by our heels. Several times we hear jackals barking, a sign of human habitation. Neither of us says a word. Each is listening to the murmurs of the night, and to all the murmurings from within. Is he, like me, straining to read what lies behind his companion's face?

We pass close by what used to be Ein Hahoresh. The orchards are still there. Nothing else is. The water tower and the dining hall, the workshops and the houses have all been reduced to dust. In the starlight, I try to detect a smirk on Mahmoud's face. Yet, after all, does it matter who has reduced Ein Hahoresh to a fine dust? Mahmoud himself might have done it, but his time has not yet come. My time hasn't come either, and I haven't even asked myself what I would like to reduce to fine dust. Maybe everything.

Rage is a poor counselor. But what else is there to keep one alive?

Once upon a time in Ein Hahoresh they conceived of a new world, a different one, but what finally came to pass was that even the old world was obliterated. Maybe the place had been swept by fury for the first and last time when even rage, like everything else, had come too late to do any good.

Do my senses betray me, is my rage numbed by grief? Do Mahmoud's senses desert him, has his heart, like mine, stopped for a moment? We walk into an ambush.

In an orange grove, of all places. I catch a bullet in the arm and roll on the ground. They are firing long bursts. Mahmoud has dropped into an irrigation basin under a tree.

I pull my urban firearm and get ready to die. After those first bursts, nothing. I try to see something, but in vain. I'm hurting. And I'm covered with blood. Behind me there's a noise: I turn and shoot without taking aim. Someone falls on top of me. I grab his submachine gun. Mahmoud has appeared by my side. I hand him the submachine gun—I can't use it with only one good arm. Mahmoud opens fire. Maybe we'll get out of here, maybe not. In an orchard an ambush squad can't consist of more than ten or so. These haven't been trained all that well. Maybe they're raw recruits. If that's the case, this must have been the baptism of fire for the one I killed. I regret it, but I'm probably a goner myself, whatever happens.

Running and crawling, we try to get out of the trap and to the edge of the orchard. There are occasional bursts of fire, a couple of grenades. And shouts and orders. We run like wounded wild beasts, drugged, dazed. What wouldn't I give for a white convertible right now.

There's an armored car in the road with all its lights out. I stop. I signal Mahmoud to do likewise.

I'm going to give myself a transfer. From the infantry to the cavalry. I don't have any grenades, but I have something that might do just as well. Mahmoud advances on the left side of the road, I on the right. If they think we're out of the orchard already, we don't stand a chance. We probably don't stand one anyway. I jump into the open car and tear-gas the driver.

Start her up, I tell Mahmoud. No lights. With one arm

that hurts and another that doesn't I heave the driver out of the car and we take off. After a few kilometers of dirt road we get to a highway.

Stop, I say. We have to close the rear doors. We get out and do it. Inside we discover quite an arsenal. Boxes of hand grenades, a bazooka and rockets, a machine gun. In the first-aid box there are bandages and disinfectant. Mahmoud cleans my wound and dresses it. There are two small holes, meaning that the bullet went right through. The important thing is that my right arm is still functional. Now I'm in the cavalry. And now what?

If I want to stay alive—never mind reaching Ein Harod, just staying alive—only some act of sheer madness can save me. Something so insane that it won't ever occur to them that anyone might try it.

I have to take some hostages.

This highway is exactly right for that, a perfect hunting ground. So what if my improbable existence is broadcast on all their radios. For a brief moment, I'm still in charge.

The best thing would be an entire busload. But are the buses running at night? Or else a private car. It doesn't matter what.

Listen, Mahmoud, let's go slowly. Look for a shoulder just before a sharp turn and park. And another thing, Mahmoud, I know you have a gun now, but you're not obliged to use it. This isn't your war.

All of a sudden, at last, there's a smirk on his face. I've been waiting for it all night long. But now it doesn't irritate me at all.

You just concentrate on killing *your* guys, he says.

After a couple of kilometers we find the right curve. Mahmoud parks the car, picks up a grenade; I have one in my pocket. We take up positions beside the car.

We don't have to wait long. God sent Jonah a fish. A military staff car sporting a long aerial slows to a halt. A uniformed brigadier general, tall, brisk, gets out and walks over to the darkened armored car.

What is going on, soldier? the general says.

Nothing, General, I say, and stick my revolver in his stomach. He looks at me in astonishment but does not lose his presence of mind.

You're an idiot, he says to me.

Yes, General, I'm an idiot. Now call your driver, please.

Oh, no.

Call him, or you're dead.

The driver is armed.

There are two of us, there's only one of him. Call him.

The general shouts, Rafi, come here.

I see, today everyone's Rafi, I say to myself.

Rafi walks up. Mahmoud points the submachine gun at him. The driver is perplexed. The general tells him, Rafi, put your hands up, we're in a fix.

Rafi, I tell Mahmoud, tie Rafi up.

Yes, Rafi, he replies.

The general cracks a smile. My name's Rafi too, he says.

How you doing, Rafi? I say to him, and Mahmoud ties up Rafi the driver. Then I tell him to tie up the general as well. There's plenty of everything in the armored car, including things to tie people up with.

Which car should we take? I ask Mahmoud.

The general's.

Mahmoud is right. The armored car must have been reported missing some time ago, but not the general's.

Where were you going, General?

You're a moron if you think I'm going to tell you anything. And just between us, let me inform you that your buddy here is an Arab. If his name is Rafi, then mine is Mahmoud.

Mahmoud, I say, tie the driver's left hand to the general's left, and then tie their right hands, and don't get confused. Then do their ankles the same way, just to make sure.

I was right about Mahmoud, says the general.

Yes, sir.

Mahmoud ties them together, and we get them both into the back seat with me next to them, gun in hand.

And now? Mahmoud asks.

Go to the armored car and get some grenades, ammo, guns, rope, the first-aid kit, and put it all in the trunk along with their guns. Get the armored car off the road and hide it, and then let's go.

The way they've been tied, they have to sit facing each other. I have a view of the driver's back and the general's face. Neither of them has anything to say.

Mahmoud comes back, gets behind the wheel. He doesn't ask me for directions. Sets off for Wadi Ara.

Turn on the radio, I tell him. He does. We hit on a pretty program of songs about Eretz Israel the Beautiful. Now I can cry if I feel like it. Someone is singing, "There was a girl from Kinereth who dwelt in Galilee." And I tell myself that this very night I have seen where they buried that girl. Under a heap of loose soil in a eucalyptus grove far from her Kinereth.

Mahmoud opens the glove compartment, takes out a pack of Kents, lights one for me and one for himself.

General, I didn't much like what you did at Ein Hahoresh. Can't say I feel much pity for you.

For your information, I was born there. So what? You do what you have to do. You shoot and you cry.

Sure, I say to myself, shoot and cry. But it's you who does the shooting, me the crying. On the radio there's another song, words by God and music by local talent.

Find something else, I tell Mahmoud. I can't listen to that.

Maybe something in Arabic?

No, thanks. Something classical, if that's all right.

Strange as it may seem, he finds me a Bach cantata. Here we are, rolling toward Wadi Ara in the company of Johann Sebastian Bach.

I've taken all kinds of trips in my life. With Johann Sebastian Bach and without. Never one like this.

Well, maybe once. That wasn't really a trip. Jerusalem, 1948. But not now. I don't want to, and I can't. Not even for myself. Yes, Vaheb by storm we conquered, not with songs, not with music, not with cantatas. And the rivers of Arnon we saw afar off but we went not thither. Even when the moon in the valley of Aijalon stood still, its dark side we saw not.

Once I traveled with Rashid right here, on the road to Wadi Ara. I asked him why he did not shed a tear for my slain child but only for his own. Many years later, I thought of the answer. The punishment we inflict on those we oppress, I told myself, is to deny them even the possibility of feeling the oppression inflicted upon others. Thus the punishment we inflict on the victim of our oppression is that we teach him how to oppress others without compunction.

You see, General, Mahmoud would like to kill me.

Why doesn't he do it?

You too would like to kill me.

That's true, but right now I can't.

Tell me, General, if you'd had this revolver in your hand back there, which one of us would you have shot first?

Mahmoud.

And you, Mahmoud, which of us two, or us three, would you have shot first?

I'm not going to tell you.

See there, says the general, I told you he's dangerous. Excuse my prying, but what is he doing with you? Or what are you doing with him?

Maybe you can answer, Mahmoud.

No. He's your general. You answer him.

All right, General. I'll tell you what we're doing. We're traveling together to find out which one of us will kill the other in the end.

Well, that sounds right, says the general, and I don't give a damn who kills who. But where are you going?

You know where, General. Ein Harod.

Ein Harod doesn't exist.

It does, and you are taking us there.

You won't get there.

With you we will.

What the hell does an Arabush have to do with Ein Harod?

Mahmoud doesn't reply. In fact, I don't know the answer to that one either. He has told me that Ein Harod is on his way. On his way where? Up to now all I know is that Mahmoud and I don't intend to kill each other. But that's all I know.

"In Thy hands, O Lord, I place my soul," sings Johann Sebastian Bach. A clear and melancholy flute accompanies him. I won't say anything, I think to myself, when I finally decide to give up my soul. I haven't given it up yet. Maybe it's getting to be time.

The general interrupts my train of thought. And you, he says, who would you shoot first?

Maybe myself, General, maybe I would shoot myself first. But I haven't made up my mind yet, so I can't really give you an answer.

When you do, let me know, the general says curtly, and I think about his childhood in Ein Hahoresh. Tell me, General, I say to him, tell me about your childhood in Ein Hahoresh.

It was great.

And yours, Mahmoud?

I didn't have one.

What about you, Mahmoud says, what was your childhood like?

You, the general says to him, you and your parents should have been finished off before you had a chance to grow up.

There's your answer, I tell Mahmoud. I haven't grown up

yet. So it really isn't too late, General, to cut me down before I do.

The call sign of the military frequency comes on. A pity. It doesn't only mean the end of our conversation, it means the end of our trip.

General, I assume that it's useless to try to force you to reply.

Affirmative.

Stop, I tell Mahmoud, this is the end of the line.

Mahmoud pulls over.

Now drive the car someplace where it won't be spotted from the air. In a few minutes they'll start looking for it.

Tell me, Arabush, are you his flunky or what?

Mahmoud turns around. His eyes are bright.

Yes, he says, and if he tells me to punch the general in the mouth, I'll punch him in the mouth.

Mahmoud starts the car and cautiously proceeds up the hill between the ravine and the rocks, taking care not to drive into the ravine or get stuck on a rock. He parks under a big leafy oak, turns off the lights, and cuts the engine.

Separate these two, I tell Mahmoud.

Well, what do you know. All this time he's been carrying a knife in his pocket. He takes it out and cuts them apart. Now the general and his driver can walk, with only their hands tied behind their backs. But I know you really have to watch out for these types. Anyone who had a great childhood in Ein Hahoresh may have surprises up his sleeve.

The general goes first. Behind him, Mahmoud. Behind Mahmoud, the driver. I bring up the rear.

Where are we going? the general wants to know.

Wherever Mahmoud tells you, General.

I see, he says. If he's taking us into an ambush, I go first.

After you, sir.

And in the starlight even the general cracks a smile.

Follow me, he says, forward march!

We proceed to ascend the stony slope.

He knows how to march. Even with his hands tied. But I'm certain he'll do his best to be seen, if at all possible. In a few minutes, they'll start lighting up the sky above us. They know his original destination. As soon as radio contact was broken, they started figuring out where he might be and sent out helicopters immediately. The rest is routine. The only factor liable to disrupt the routine is Mahmoud. Into Thy hands, Lord, I won't yet give up my soul. For the moment I'm sharing it between the two of you, Rafi and Mahmoud, and let God decide.

Not that I'm forgetting the driver. It's true that he doesn't seem quite as alert. But many have died from underestimating someone. Walking behind him, I am alert. Well, as alert as I can be, friend. My wounded arm is no help.

It hasn't taken them long to figure it out. Here they are, right above our heads. We can hear them clearly. Down come the flares, and the little wood is bathed in light. I don't think they have found the hidden staff car yet. In no time there'll be ground vehicles, and their drivers will follow the tire tracks, discover the car, estimate the time elapsed and our possible position, and the rest will be routine. Time for some faster than fast thinking.

The driver catches me by surprise. All of a sudden he bounds into the air, spins and kicks backward, catching me in the balls—where else? I fall down.

Mahmoud doesn't fire. He simply pushes the muzzle of his submachine gun into the general's back and whispers, Don't move.

Can you get up? he asks me.

Yes.

Keep an eye on your general.

I point my gun at him.

Mahmoud walks over to the driver. Lie down on your back, he tells him.

The driver sits down on the ground, then stretches out on his back.

Mahmoud jumps on him with both feet, trampling his balls.

I won't forget this, says the general.

For a moment I think I'll make him lie down too so I can jump on his balls. No. I won't forget this either.

Now get up, says Mahmoud.

The driver gets up again. We resume our march in the same order: the general in front, Mahmoud behind him, followed by the driver and me. Where are we going, where will we get to, will we have time to get out of here? I also won't forget Mahmoud. Live and learn. I'm still learning.

Like quite a few Israelis, I am an amateur archeologist. Although I'm a city dweller, over the years I have learned to read the language of the land and to understand what it tells me. Understanding the land isn't just Kipling or Jim Corbett stuff, like knowing when the tiger is right behind you. Understanding the land means knowing where human beings have been, how they lived, what they did, and how they dealt with their problems.

There's a groove in the rock. I know those grooves. They are man-made. Some ancient stonecutter made them in order to channel rainwater into a well. In Eretz Israel, water has always been a problem. Every drop counts. The stonecutter knew which slope the rain would run down when it fell, and he knew just how to use gravity to channel it from the slope to the well he had dug in the ground. There was a groove here, and there would be an old well.

Follow the groove, I tell the general.

I see it, he says.

It isn't just a well we find. It is a town. Maybe not exactly a town, but a sanctuary for a lot of people. An entire village of rebels must have taken shelter here once. When? In the days of Ramses, perhaps. Maybe later, at the time of the Maccabees. Or the Romans, or even later. Was there ever a time when there weren't rebels here? Or refugees? Was there ever a time when people didn't go underground until things blew over? And had they blown over? Would they ever?

It isn't easy to get in: a great boulder has been rolled across the well's mouth.

Untie them!

Mahmoud obeys. I let the three of them move the boulder. I wonder who last put it back there. We enter, but in a slightly altered order: the general, his driver, Mahmoud, and me last, lighting the way for all of us with the flashlight held in my good hand. Inside there's a slope. We have to slide down on our backsides. At the end of the slope we find a tunnel, high enough to walk in if we crouch. At the end of that there are steps cut into the rock. Obviously, none of us is able to replace the boulder at the entrance, not that there would have been any point in doing so. We haven't come here to die. At least not all of us, I hope. Whoever survives will be able to get out again.

At the end of the steps there is a large room carved into the rock. Not the place for us to stay. At the other end of the room there is a narrow opening. We enter it and find another sloping tunnel, really a kind of gallery: first we slide downward, then we have to climb. At the end of this gallery there is a small room. We'll stay here.

We must conserve the flashlight—we'll have to leave here before the batteries are gone. I tell Mahmoud, Tie them up like mummies.

Mahmoud ties them up like mummies. He loops the rope around them, including arms and legs, so that they look like sausages. Then he ties them together to make one great big mummy.

It's almost day, and I'm wiped out. No need to count sheep. You can count people who've been killed, count places that used to exist but are no longer there, everything that once was and no longer is. Not even my aching arm can keep me awake. How sweet the sleep of the fugitive who has found yet one more shelter for yet another night underground.

Mahmoud wakes me up.

It's noon already, he says. We have to decide what to do. How's the arm?

Better.

In a day or two it'll all be over.

What about us?

It may all be over for us too, says Mahmoud.

Why don't you pipe down, there are people trying to sleep, says the general.

Good morning, General, I say. Did you have a good night's rest? How are you this morning?

My bladder is bursting.

Mahmoud, if it's not too much trouble, why don't you untie them and let them go relieve themselves one at a time.

How long are we going to stay here?

Quite a while.

That's what I was afraid of. What are we going to eat?

I don't know. But I think we'll have enough water. We have to start looking for the well. It might be at the end of the tunnel leading out of this room.

Mahmoud separates the general from the driver. The driver, followed by Mahmoud, goes first to piss in the big room.

I have a proposal to make, says the general.

Trucks for blood?

Sort of. You kill Mahmoud and you'll get off with life.

For killing him?

Very funny. For that you wouldn't even get a day. What else should we do with them? The prisons are packed with them, and they're just getting fatter there.

Why life, and why Mahmoud?

Because I don't want this story to get out. It wouldn't help matters.

Tell me more, I'm listening.

You're dead, you know. So instead of being dead, you'll be alive. The story won't get out. But we can't have some Mahmoud around who's seen an Israeli brigadier general taken prisoner. Especially not one who's tied up an Israeli general like a sausage. If he talks, that isn't good for the Jews.

For which Jews?

The Jews, *c'est moi.*

I used to be one too.

Maybe so. But that was when you were alive. You're a dead man now. Let's say you're a dead *Jew*, if that makes you feel better.

There's some obscure logic to that, I say to myself. Just like the only good Arab is a dead Arab, the only bad Jew is a dead one.

General, I'll have to think it over. It's an interesting proposition, but there are lots of angles to consider.

How long does it take that asshole to shit? And speaking of assholes, if it's all the same to you, I want you to come along when it's my turn, instead of Mahmoud. I don't need him seeing a Hebrew brigadier general's ass on top of everything else.

All of a sudden I remember the ass I never got to see in that white convertible. Surely she is an angel by now.

Mahmoud and the driver come back.

Tie him up again, I say. I'm going to take Mirza here out for a leak.

Time to walk the dog, the general says with a sneer, but there's a note of cheer in his voice, and I realize that he's beginning to enjoy the situation and that I have to be careful with him, very careful.

Mahmoud has tied the driver up like a mummy again. I go out with the general. We crawl through the tunnel to the large room. He turns to face me and takes a leak. Then he drops his pants and hunkers down, still facing me.

You won't see it either, he says. And think about my offer. You don't have much of a choice. Besides, you look to me like someone who has killed some Arabs in his time.

I don't respond. What can I say? The general takes a shit.

Let me tell you a story, I say. Once in the Cyrenaica desert there was a British sergeant everybody hated. One night he goes out into the dunes to take a shit. Someone sneaks up behind him with a shovel and steals his turd. When he's buttoned up again and turns to look, he goes out of his gourd and has to be taken to the hospital. He was discharged.

The session's over, says the general, and stands up. We can go now. And by the way, you can have mine as a present. You can even eat it if you want.

The session isn't over. It's hardly begun. Why did you say that Ein Harod no longer exists?

Because it doesn't.

What have you done to Ein Harod?

Nothing.

That's not what the radio said.

So ask the radio, don't ask me. Let me tell you, it's no use going there. First of all, you won't get there, and second, there won't be anything there when you do. In the third place, I've made you an offer that none of your colleagues got. Instead of being dead, you won't be.

First you said they surrendered. Now you say they're dead.

Only those who didn't surrender.

Listen, General, and listen closely: you'll take me to Ein Harod, you and no one else. And I'll get there alive, because if I don't, you'll never get anywhere alive again.

You listen to me, you poor lost soul. You have a gun, but you're in a worse bind than I am. I stand a chance: either I manage to escape, or you come to your senses and accept my offer. You don't stand a chance at all.

I hear you. Now tell me, why Ein Hahoresh?

Because they forgot what that Greek wrote. That everything is war.

But at Ein Harod they didn't forget.

They forgot who to fight and who not to. And now I think you'll agree that the session is over.

After you, General.

We go back to the small room. Mahmoud ties the general up like a mummy and then ties him to the driver again in one handy package.

Let's go find the well, I say to Mahmoud. We leave. He walks ahead, I follow with the flashlight. At the far end of the room is a narrow opening we haven't noticed before. After squeezing through it, we find ourselves in a tunnel almost as tall as a man.

It is an enormous well, and very deep. And full of water. Water that is perhaps two thousand years old, maybe even older—more like five thousand years.

From the edge of the well, stone steps lead to the bottom. There is even a little light from God knows where. Perhaps there's a crack in the rock. Here Egyptians have hidden from Hittites, Canaanites from Israelites, and the sons of Israel from all the others. Who knows, maybe ten surviving warriors sat here once throwing dice to decide who would take whose life and who would remain alone to kill himself. Who knows, one day excavations might uncover an inscribed pottery shard, the skeleton of a warrior with his sword and spear, some ritual objects, and all those final bits of testimony to the condition of a man about to die. Probably no other country in the world is as rich in such testimony. But here I am not the excavator, I am the find of the future.

We lower our canteens into the well and drink. Then we refill them and take them back to our, shall we say, prisoners. Hard to believe, but they're our prisoners, mine and Mahmoud's.

We lift them up, one of us holding them, the other pouring

water into their mouths, first the driver, then the general. Then we lay them back down together.

Mahmoud goes to relieve himself, then I do too. The way of all flesh. Then, cigarette in mouth, silence. Stream of thoughts.

Listen, Mahmoud, we have to find out what the weather's like outside.

I've been thinking about that.

If it's been raining, our tracks have been wiped out. But if it hasn't been raining, they'll follow them and we'll be surrounded.

Is that good or bad?

I don't know. But first we have to find out.

How do you know whether I'll be raven or dove?

That remains to be seen.

All right. While I'm gone, you can be nice to your prisoners.

Mahmoud leaves.

Now I can reflect upon the subject of Mahmoud and myself.

He isn't very talkative, nor does he volunteer much information. Me either. And neither one of us is in a particularly jovial mood. He has obviously eluded the curfew. And if people like me can't travel on the roads, things are a hundred times worse for someone like him. If they're shooting my kind down like mad dogs, what must they be doing to people like him?

If all the villages are under curfew, he must be trying to go much farther than Ein Harod. Someplace where we aren't the law. As long as both of us are running for our lives, I have no reason to worry about him. Nor do I have any reason to confide in him. When hatred overcomes reason, Comrade Uzi has the floor. And who among those who have chosen to take up arms has never shot anybody nice?

Mahmoud comes back after a short while. See, he says, the

dove has returned to the ark. Out there it's the flood. Not a chance they'll find us. No scout, no dog, nobody.

Good, that takes care of that. Now tell me why you came back.

Because I enjoy your company and because I like living in caves.

Oh, yeah. Tell me more.

Because you need me.

That sounds interesting. Why?

For the same reason I need you. I may be useful to you in getting you past the Arabs, but I can't get past the Jews without you. You and your general, you are my visa.

Visa to where?

Freedom.

Where's that, freedom?

It's where you fight for it.

Why don't you fight here?

I have fought, and lost.

You haven't fought. You weren't even born when you lost.

That's true. I lost even before I was born.

You know who threw you out? Me.

You're one of them?

What do you think?

You hate us that much?

I had no choice.

Why are you telling me this?

To tell the truth.

You're not telling the truth. To say you had no choice, that's not telling the truth.

Why do you sodomize Jewesses and call yourself Rafi?

Because that's what you've done to us.

You made us throw you out.

Liar.

We have a right to a place.

It's ours.

Next to you.

There's nothing like that in the real world. In the real world it's either/or.

No, there is something like that in the real world, there isn't just either/or.

Under the ground maybe.

That's where we are now, underground. And that reminds me of the second problem. Food. I still have a little bit of what I've been carrying. But not enough for four.

At daybreak there's rabbits.

They know what area we're in, and they're all around us, day and night, and at dawn when you shoot a rabbit, they'll shoot you.

I can get them with a stone. Besides, I can catch some partridges.

How?

They sleep in nooks in the rocks at night. You can catch them by hand, one in each hand. I used to do it when I was a kid.

I believe him. Not because I'm gullible but because I once saw someone do exactly that at night. Crawl up to a rock like a snake and grab two sleeping partridges, one in each hand. I believe him about the rabbits too.

From now until dawn we have plenty of time. We can use it. I use it by staying flat on my back and thinking things over. Our two prisoners can't use theirs quite as well, but they survive. Mahmoud uses his time to annoy me. He proceeds to sing a song with about a hundred and nineteen verses, with each verse lasting at least five minutes. Not that I listen to it all. From time to time I have to go check on the prisoners. They need water, they need to take a leak. The water's no problem. For the leaks I need Mahmoud's assistance, which also gives me a break from his song. At about two in the morning Mahmoud goes out hunting.

He returns with two partridges. We pluck them, make a fire, wake the prisoners and untie their hands, then sit down to eat, all four of us. Suddenly I'm reminded of fires and feasts in the past, and for a moment I feel like raising my voice and singing with my two prisoners those songs we used to like about the things we used to like.

Mahmoud has also brought back some herbs and makes tea. For a moment I forget where I am, who I'm with, and why. It's almost pleasant.

Get some sleep, Mahmoud, I say. When you wake up, it's my turn.

Mahmoud goes to sleep and stops singing for two hours. Now, if I wanted to, I could sing with the two Rafis, the two well-trussed Rafis.

I could sing, "On the barricades we'll meet again, we'll meet again, on the barricades we'll raise liberty aloft by means of blood and fire."

That used to be my song. But I've had it with liberty by means of blood and fire. Here's the blood and here's the fire, but where's liberty?

That, more or less, is what Isaac asked his father Abraham: here's the fire, here's the wood, but where's the lamb for the holocaust?

"On the banks of the rivers of Babylon," I sing silently to myself, "there we sat down and wept, remembering Zion."

No one joins me in that one. Mahmoud wakes up and comes to relieve me. I go and doze off for a while. I count a hundred and nineteen lambs for the holocaust, and that does it.

Some time later I open my eyes with a headache and a sense of unease. Something seems wrong, and it has been bothering me in my sleep. What is it?

Good thing you're awake, says Mahmoud. Your prisoners have to take a leak.

Mahmoud unties them and walks off with the driver. I stay there with the general. I don't feel like talking to him, so I don't. I smoke a cigarette. Mahmoud comes back with the driver. Take the general too, I tell him, I want to sit here and think things over.

I sit there and think things over. Mahmoud comes back.

You know, he says to me with a smile, I just got a very interesting offer. But I turned it down.

Why?

Because if the offer was any good, he would have made it to you first.

Right you are, I tell him, if it was any good, he would have made it to me first. And that reminds me of a problem I'm having. I want to get rid of the driver.

Why's that? Two is better than one.

On the contrary. One is better. With two of them here, they may be able to set each other free. Besides, I need him to go out there. So untie him.

Mahmoud looks at me, astonished, and asks, You're sure?

I'm sure. Get on with it.

Mahmoud unties the driver. You're free, I tell him, so get out of here.

I won't go. I won't abandon the general.

You won't be abandoning him. You'll leave and you'll walk, and you'll tell them that he is in my hands and that I'll let him go, alive, but only if I'm guaranteed safe passage to Ein Harod.

With this Arabush?

With him, yes, but not with you, if you don't mind.

I'm not going. Go ahead, kill me.

I'll do no such thing. If you won't go, I'll tie you up again and pound your head until you pass out, and when you come to, I'll throw some water on you and pound your head some more until you pass out again, and in the end you'll do as I say, so why not just start now?

Go on, Rafi, says the general. He's such a shit, he'll really do that to you.

But, General, you've been so polite to me until now.

Even when I was polite to you, you were a piece of shit. Now you're an asshole as well. If you're hiding, why do you want to be found again? And if you really want to be found, why are you hiding here?

You're right, General, I've been a stupid asshole. I thought that I was hiding to avoid being found. I didn't realize that I was hiding so they'd know exactly where I am, and with whom. I want them to know that I've got you, and I want them to know that they can get into this cave only one at a time and that anyone forcing his way in will be killed until they've had enough of that. And I want them to negotiate with me for your head.

They won't do it.

Oh, but they will, they will. You're going to scream and whimper and tell them that we've already cut off one ear and are about to start on your nose, and then your tongue, and then ear number two.

You're not going to do that, and I won't scream.

Yes, I will, and you'll scream all right. So shut up, you know it's true.

You'd really be able to do that? With the Arabush here?

I haven't told you yet what I saw at dusk one night in a eucalyptus grove. Well, what I saw there, I for one couldn't bring myself to do that. So good luck, and I hope you make it home safe and sound. If you want, you can write something for Rafi to take with him.

Not a word. You really are a shit. You know what you've done, you've done me out of a good lay. I had a rendezvous with this very pretty girl from Ein Harod.

I don't know why, but I fly into a rage. Perhaps that's what he's been wanting me to do. Or perhaps it's because out of all the talents humanity has endowed me with, this is the only one left. I punch him in the stomach with all the strength I can muster. But his stomach is hard, well trained. He just takes one step back. His smile is far from pleasant.

You're going to pay for this too, he says, and you'll pay for the fuck I missed.

I burst into tears.

What have they done to us, what have they done to us, what has become of us, and where has it all gone? And yet it could have been different. Everything could have been different. Me too, I could have been different.

Mahmoud looks at me with a bitter smile, as if he has read my thoughts: It's too late for you to remember how to cry. How many villages have you wiped off the face of the earth without shedding a tear? We were the only ones crying then.

You're wrong, Mahmoud. The only thing it's too late to do is to be born. It's never too late to cry.

Then I say to the general, All right, you tell the driver to go, with or without a letter. I'm willing to turn you over alive if I get a safe conduct to Ein Harod. First of all, they have to send me a radio transmitter and some food, here to this cave. Because if we're reduced to eating human flesh, you'll be the first to go. Now tell him to get going, goddamn it.

Rafi gives me the look of one who won't forget and goes.

Silence descends. Half an hour later we hear voices through a loudspeaker.

We're sending a radio and some food. Don't fire on the messenger, it's an Arab prisoner.

What a sense of humor. The radio arrives, along with a sackful of combat rations. But the messenger is not what we think, not that I would have fired anyway. It's a girl, a girl from Ein Harod.

Well, Rafi, she says, what's going on? She shines her flashlight on us.

She's nicely built, wearing jeans and a light sweater.

See for yourself.

You know I've been waiting for you all night.

I didn't come. What did you do?

What could I do? I tried to console myself.

Me too.

Excuse me, I say. If I understand this right, you are from Ein Harod?

That depends on which one you mean, the A or the B village. I'm from the B.

What's happened down there?

No one's told me.

Did she shudder? I watch her closely. A pretty face, a clear look. She rushes her words a little. Her brown hair is lank. I think she's noticed my look.

And who is that? she asks, pointing at Mahmoud.

Well, I'm the Arabush, says Mahmoud.

You don't look like an Arab at all.

What do I look like?

You look like someone who won't look like anything at all in no time, and that's a promise, says the general.

Will you stop that, says the girl. No one's even asked me my name. Listen, Rafi, that's not very polite, you should have introduced me.

This is Liora, Liora from Ein Harod.

Give me that sack, I say. We're hungry.

She opens it and takes out the combat rations.

Tie her up, I tell Mahmoud. He does. I notice a slight tremor in his hands. What do you know. He finishes. All right, now untie the general. Mahmoud obeys, but his hands are still trembling. What do you know.

The rations come with a can opener. Do the honors, I tell the general.

The general does the honors. Not even glancing at us, he eats his share. The corned beef, the olives, the halvah, the jam, the crackers, all of it. Then he says, I'm thirsty.

I pick up another ration and offer it to Mahmoud. He opens it and hands it back to me. No, I say, you eat first, and when you're done you can go get some water.

You didn't have to tie me up, says the girl. Her name is Liora, but I'm not used to that yet. For me she's always the girl, the girl from Ein Harod. You didn't have to tie me up, I wouldn't have run away. I came here in good faith.

And I've tied you up in bad faith.

Mahmoud returns with the water and gives our general a drink. I open my ration and eat it. After Rafi has had his drink, Mahmoud ties him up again.

Should we tie them together?

Yes, I say, tie them up into one big mummy. Then we'll talk to them. But first I'll talk to the outside.

I pick up the radio, press the button, say, This is Free Ein Harod, over.

This is the general of the Northern Command, answers a voice in the instrument. Identify yourself.

I just did.

Give me your name.

That is my name. Free Ein Harod is my name, and that's where I want to go, to Free Ein Harod.

There's no such thing, Mr. Free Ein Harod, no such thing. I advise you to surrender. You'll get a fair trial.

I'm not alone.

We know. You're with the Arabush. Our offer applies to you. We have no offer for the Arabush.

Go fuck yourself, general of the Northern Command, sir.

You're mistaken, it's you who's fucked. I repeat: surrender and you'll have a fair trial. That's all I have to say to you.

I repeat: I'm not alone, and you know it. I have one of your brigadier generals here with me.

One less. The best die first.

Then there's the girl.

You're breaking my heart, but you can't make an omelet without breaking some eggs, you know.

What do I have to cut off this general first to show you I mean business?

You can start with his dick, for all I care.

All right, I'll talk to you in a couple of minutes, over.

I'm suddenly very hot and have trouble breathing. I

unbutton my shirt. The girl looks at me with an amused expression.

Under your shirt you're old, she says.

I know, I tell her. I'm only young under my pants.

I think of a lot of things but drive those thoughts from my mind. The first thing is to stay alive. Everything else later. If at all.

Oh, God, where am I and what is all this? I'll pass through this, I'll pass through all of this like a knife through butter. I won't hear any of it, and I'll arrive in Ein Harod, and I'll get there alive, not dead, because the dead cannot praise God, not the dead, oh, God. There, I've spoken the Name. That's the start. Who knows, soon I may be able to say, Into Thy hands, Lord.

I pick up the radio again. This is Free Ein Harod.

The answer is immediate. This is the general of the Northern Command. Have you decided to surrender?

No, General, I haven't. I'm giving you an hour to tell me when and how I'll receive my safe conduct to Ein Harod before I cut off what you suggested.

Give me that thing, my general says.

I knew it. I split the mummy up into two separate mummies, then I untie his hands but not his feet and hand him the radio.

Brigadier General Rafi here, over.

General of the Northern Command, over.

General, he'll do it.

So?

So, that's not too great.

Well, what can I do?

I'll tell you what you can do, sir. You know the one about the fellow who went to the dentist? The dentist puts him in the chair and picks up the drill, and the guy grabs the dentist by the balls and says, Now I hope we understand each other.

Nice story. So?

I'm holding your balls right now, and you know exactly what I'm talking about.

All right, we understand each other.

You wouldn't want me to tell what I know. You wouldn't want these Arabushes to hear it.

So what do you want?

I want to get out of here.

What if I let him cut you up and we sort things out later?

We won't be sorting anything out. It's later already.

I have my orders. You know the orders too. No negotiations. I couldn't get it approved.

Call the chief of staff. Or let me talk to him.

We can't reach him at this time. And if it's the prime minister you want, we can't reach him either. Give me that Arabush shit from Ein Harod.

I take the receiver.

Listen, you—and you heard what I called you—as far as I'm concerned you can go ahead and cut off whatever you want whenever you like. I can't give you any kind of answer before seven o'clock tomorrow morning. I have no authority, and at this time it isn't possible to get in touch with the chief of staff or the prime minister or the minister of defense. Don't ask me where they are or why, it's none of your business. I'm authorized to accept your surrender, nothing else. You'll get an answer tomorrow morning at seven if you're still around, and I hope you won't be. Over and out.

I turn off the radio. General Rafi stares at me pensively. Listen, he says, I have to talk to you in private.

I think about that for a minute. The minute is over. I tie his hands behind his back again and untie his legs. I tell him to walk ahead of me.

Don't trust me alone with her, says Mahmoud. I'm an Arab, you know.

Listen, tell her your name is Rafi and stick it up her ass, okay?

For a moment Mahmoud's face freezes, and I'm afraid he'll

do something stupid. But then he smiles and says, You know, in the underground I'm Mahmoud.

Walk ahead of me, I tell the general.

We go into the big latrine room. What is it you want to say to me? I ask him.

You don't know that son of a whore. I do.

To me, you're all sons of whores. Besides, I certainly do know him. As if we'd been sucking on the same tit.

You know what he has in mind. You don't stand a chance.

What do you suggest?

I'll take you to Ein Harod.

Why? To save me from that son of a whore?

To save all of us.

Tell me when you're lying.

Always.

So what you told me about Ein Harod was a pack of lies.

I didn't say that. You know the story about the Cretan who said that all Cretans were liars?

So even what you're saying now is a lie.

I didn't say that. See above.

Let me think it over.

You haven't got much time.

Don't tell me how much time I have. I have my whole life ahead of me.

Your whole life, sure, except it ain't what it used to be.

Let's go back, I say. I have to think about it.

We go back. Mahmoud is sitting next to the tied-up girl, smoking a cigarette.

Hope you had a good time.

Just lovely. Considering I'm tied up, really lovely, thanks. He's been telling me about his village.

He's never told me about it.

Maybe you never asked him.

You're right, I tell her, maybe it's because I never asked. Mahmoud, be so kind as to tie our general up and untie the girl.

With pleasure, says Mahmoud, and thanks for everything.

Mahmoud tied and untied.

I hope you're more comfortable now and we can go have a
little talk. You first.

She gets up and walks ahead, surefooted as if she'd grown
up in a cave.

We don't go to the big latrine room but to the well. Why
don't you sit down here at the edge and start talking, I say.

I think you'd like to go to bed with me.

Tell me about Ein Harod.

I told you.

The truth.

That is the truth. I told you, no one has told me anything.
Maybe it's because my parents are there. I left the kibbutz
some time ago.

When?

Don't ask me, I don't want to talk about it. It hurts.

I want to know what hurts you.

Not true. You haven't asked Mahmoud what hurts him.
What hurts him is me. Tell me about Rafi.

What's to tell?

You're his lover or his concubine or what?

You want to know if I sleep with him. The answer is yes.
What else do you want to know about me?

Why did they decide to send you here?

I don't know. For no reason. It's none of my business.

What exactly is your business?

This may sound corny, but what I've always liked to do
most is live a little. And now everything seems so totally
impossible. And you, you look so lost.

I want to tell her that she looks a little lost too, but I
decide against it. She says nothing either, so we both say
nothing.

I feel like taking a swim, she says suddenly. Look how
clear the water is.

She takes her clothes off. Jumps into the water naked. Don't you want to come in? she asks me.

Not yet, I say, not yet.

Goddamn, she's really beautiful. Every one of us knows what that is, a beautiful body. It's beautiful skin, smooth, tanned; it's lovely, harmonious movements. She is a nymph, a daughter of the forest and the wellspring, and I, what the hell am I? Here and now, right at this moment, I don't even want to know what the hell I am.

She comes out of the water, climbs up on the edge of the well, and sits down close to me. Wet, shivering a little from the cold. They're not going to do this to me, I tell myself, not to me. I keep my distance. She doesn't try to come any closer. She sits there, shivering, a few meters away.

I don't know how long we sit like that. I haven't looked up, but it seems to me that the little bit of light that filters in here somehow has grown dimmer. Or perhaps it's something inside of me that's grown dimmer.

*It is good that your hand still grasps our heart*
*Don't pity it when it grows tired of running*
*Don't let it go dim like a room*
*Without the stars that have been left outside.*

Ancient poem from the ancient days of my youth.

I have no idea what will come of all this. Nor do I know whether it makes any sense. I have lived an entire life here in this underground place that has grown dim, and perhaps a second of eternity beyond that. You can come now, all of you, to pick me up and carry me over to the other side.

She is drying off. She has stopped shivering. If this were Paradise, she would be Eve before the Tree of Knowledge. She looks at me without the least shadow of a smile and says, You sure you don't want to make love to me?

I didn't say I don't want to.

Tell me something.

Once, I say, we arrived at a spring just before dawn. It

was still dark all around, a pale sliver of moon was touching the hillside. The birds were waking up, starting their song. I was lying on my back looking at the treetops. And that'll never happen again, never.

She says nothing.

As if I wouldn't like to tell her. As if I wouldn't have liked to tell myself throughout all these years. My wife says I repress those things. Maybe. But I know one thing. I know that the one who wakes up stops running, and I still have to run, in the light of those stars that have been left outside.

Don't say anything now, I say to Liora. I have to think about something.

I just know, have known all this time, that something very important is nagging me.

Rafi. He hasn't been lying, he knows them. They've said they'll give us an answer at seven in the morning, that they have no authority to do anything or even to consult anyone before then. A lie. I know them. This very moment they're preparing an assault. If they don't have a map of this cave, they'll get hold of one. I'm sure they have it already. It's their business to know everything, aboveground, underground, and everywhere else. That's what they're getting paid for, for knowing everything. And they'll attack at dawn, that's their method. After having lulled me to sleep with their promises, reassuring me and giving me the illusion that I'm in control. I have to, I have to find out right now whether there's another entrance to this cave and whether it has any branch tunnels. And if there is such an entrance, it'll be my exit. When they mount their assault at dawn, they mustn't find me here. I don't stand a chance here, I have to be somewhere else by then.

But where? And why is Rafi willing to take me to Ein Harod? And if they're really familiar with this cave, why doesn't Rafi know it? And why is the general of the Northern Command ready to sacrifice Rafi at this point? Is Rafi such a menace to him, and if so, why exactly? And why is Rafi willing to go so far as to take me to Ein Harod? Is he, like me, suddenly lost?

Put your clothes on, I say, we have things to do.

She gets dressed. Quickly but without haste.

Walk in front of me, I'll light the way. From the well room itself there is no other exit but the way we came in. But where's the light coming from? Probably from above. I shine the flashlight on the ceiling. Nothing. I decide to retrace our steps. She walks on, I follow, shining the light into every niche in the rock wall, into every turn of the gallery.

I find it.

There's a stone slab on top of something that looks like a sarcophagus. She helps me lift the slab, and it isn't a sarcophagus. At the bottom there's actually a vertical shaft going down about two meters. And at the end of the shaft I can see an opening.

I tell her to get in. She jumps and slides into the hole. I jump after her. She is crawling ahead of me. The tunnel is narrow and suffocating. After some twenty meters it grows wider and we can stand up. We proceed along a long, twisting corridor. Good God, it must be two hundred meters long. Part of it has to be natural—who would have been crazy enough to hack through all this rock?

We come to a fork. I decide to try the right side first. In happier days, I would have been bowled over by what I see.

It is a huge suite of five rooms with cellars full of amphorae. I don't open them. There's also a synagogue with its ritual bath. On the synagogue wall is a bas-relief of the menorah with its seven candles.

No skeletons, no tragic vestiges of a last stand. Not even you, my beauty, with your braids and your sandals showing off your slender ankles, caught in a final embrace against the ribs of the man who was me. Perhaps they had managed to escape.

We retrace our steps to the fork and take the left turn. Liora's hair isn't braided, and it isn't the season for sandals.

But her braids and her sandals waiting in a cave in the Judean desert for eighteen centuries—they are my homeland, and I'm telling this to you too, Mahmoud, even if you can't hear me now.

Tell me, Liora, who is Rafi?

You've never heard of people falling in love by chance?

If you love him, why did you proposition me?

Here, underground, everything up there loses its meaning.

Who is Rafi up there?

A man I loved, up there.

And now?

Now there is no more up there. Now everything is down here.

We'll get out of here, Liora, and we'll go up there again and stay there forever. Walk ahead of me.

In this tunnel, our progress is less exhausting. It is possible to walk in a crouch. After twenty meters or so the tunnel grows wider and becomes a corridor. But at the end of that there's another goddamned fork. This is getting more and more complicated, but perhaps that's just as well. At least I know now which direction they won't be coming from. If that synagogue and ritual bath had ever been discovered, the whole country would have been talking about it.

Once again I turn to the right, we go on walking, and suddenly we see the stars. Yes, the sky, the starry sky. So here's an exit. I turn back, take the left fork. A tunnel, a corridor, and at the end of it, a large room. And some cellars. Big, beautiful amphorae, intact. No exit.

Come with me, I tell her. I walk back to where I saw the starlight. Out, I say.

She climbs out and I follow her. We're in a hollow, not a very deep one. There is a big fig tree. Figs like graves, brooks, and caves.

I crawl to the edge of the hollow and look out. Silence. Sky. An oak wood. The fig tree gives us cover. Thanks, fig tree.

The ground is damp and warm, I grab a handful of soil. I am going to get to Ein Harod, I am going to get there.

Suddenly I feel like making love to her. Here, under the fig tree, under the sky full of stars, on the wet ground. I've never been one of those heroes who restrain their desires, but this time I do. Not here, not now.

We'll go back now, I say.

Let's just go, she says, let's get out of here right now. I'll take you to Ein Harod.

Can't do that, I tell her. I still owe Mahmoud.

You owe him underground. You don't owe him anything aboveground.

I owe him everywhere.

She says nothing. We go back.

There is a story by Kafka about some kind of animal that digs a tunnel to hide from its enemy. It fills the tunnel with sufficient provisions to sustain a siege. When all its preparations have been made, it goes out to see if the enemy has really come and if he'll really try to invade the tunnel.

Not so dumb, actually, that beast of Kafka's. If you're going to die, why not do it under the open sky? Come on, I say to the general and Mahmoud, we're leaving.

Where to? the general wants to know.

To a picnic under a fig tree. Untie his legs. We have to get going right now. And don't leave any grenades behind, we'll need them.

For a moment I think about mining the first entrance.

Don't do what you're thinking about, the general says.

And I don't. He's right. It's almost midnight. We replace the slab on the sarcophagus and go on out through that hollow by the fig tree.

We set out, the general first, Mahmoud behind him, then the girl, and me bringing up the rear. Between the hollow and the oak wood lies dead land surrounded by hills with no movement or sign of life. If they plan to surround us before even launching an assault, this is the moment to slip out of the noose with utmost dispatch. We run fast, bent over, and reach the oaks.

We are now on a high plateau with a line of hills at the far end. We can get there before dawn. After a silent march we reach the rise of the first hill, scramble up, and find ourselves in another small oak wood.

With total precision, the attack comes at five in the morning. There is a faint glimmer of dawn. As I predicted, they don't know about the exit any more than they know about the synagogue or any of those treasures of the past that in happier days would have filled their hearts with excitement, pride, and pain. We hear the explosions and the shots, we see the flares, and we even catch whiffs of smoke and the tear gas they have blown into the cave before moving in.

Will they discover the sarcophagus that isn't a sarcophagus and follow us here? But why would they want to do that, anyway? Soon the sun will rise, and we are surrounded in any case, so all they have to do is to tighten the noose slowly and methodically until they find us, and then we'll be in a pocket and they'll just wipe us out.

No more explosions, no more shots. Silence. There's even a bird singing somewhere. The radio begins to crackle.

We've identified you, says the voice of the general of the Northern Command, we know who you are. We also have a surprise for you.

Papa! It's me! Can you hear me?

It's the voice of my eldest son. He is eleven years old. I named him after my father. And now it's the voice of my little girl. Seven. Papa, she says, come with us. Golden hair and blue eyes she has.

If you don't give us your coordinates and come out in the open with your hands up, the whole gang, we'll start by killing the girl. You have five minutes.

I don't answer.

You have no choice. You're surrounded anyway, and we'll

take you in half an hour at the most. Don't you have any pity for your children? Is it their fault?

I don't answer. Five minutes pass. We hear a volley.

I see Liora's mouth open to cry out, and I slap my hand over it, almost stifling her. Mahmoud's eyes look like they're popping out of their sockets. He has grabbed the sub-machine gun and rammed it into the general's stomach. Don't do anything stupid now, I tell him. This isn't your fight.

The voice comes over the radio again. You have five more minutes, and if I don't see you with your hands up, or hear you at least, that's it for your boy as well.

I don't say anything. Five long minutes go by. Then the voice comes back.

Your bluffing won't work. We know you're around here somewhere. Thanks for the synagogue, by the way. You have exactly ten seconds to make a sound. And don't think we'll hesitate. Just count to ten.

Ten seconds pass. Another volley.

Everybody up, I tell Mahmoud. Let's go.

Where?

To Ein Harod. Get going.

We move off, the general first, Mahmoud behind him, then the girl and me. Liora moves in a daze, like a sleep-walker. I know what's going on in her head. What can I tell her?

The oak wood runs along the slope of a narrow, shallow ravine, and we hurry down into it. We have cover, at least for the time being. Whatever the Northern Command general's next move, in the shelter of this ravine they can only get us in hand to hand combat. We sit down.

I have to think.

I'm not that callous yet. Or maybe I am, I don't know. I don't know how I would have reacted if I had thought they were really going to kill my children. But I knew, I just knew they wouldn't do it. Not because they are tenderhearted, but simply because it would be pointless. They'll get me sooner or later, and it's not their way to commit an irreversible act sooner if they can just as well do it later. No child in this world can be killed twice.

Not that I haven't made some mistakes. Maybe I shouldn't have gone into the cave, maybe I shouldn't have sent the driver out, maybe I shouldn't have left the cave. But in my situation I don't have time not to make mistakes. The little time I have has to be entirely devoted to correcting one mistake with another as quickly as possible.

I think about my father. Black hair, green eyes. And I think about my mother. When they were alive, I never asked them what to do. But now that they're dead I want to tell them what I'm thinking of doing.

I have this old photograph. Papa is holding me in his arms, Mama next to him with the baby carriage. There's a happy expression in his eyes. A young father full of pride. But there's something else too. It's the look of a man with a purpose and a reason for living. The look of a rebel who grabs History with both hands and squeezes until it surrenders. My mother's blue eyes seem softer. But I know that people with that look have been burned at the stake, never renouncing their faith.

I also have a photograph of myself holding my son in my arms. I too look happy, but that's all, there is none of my father's other expression in my eyes. I don't grab History by the throat, it's the other way around. My wife looks gentle and pensive, and I know she has a secret, but I don't know what it is.

Now, Papa, I tell my father in my heart, now it's me too. And listen, Mama, your son has become a rebel.

One minute the world is silent. The next, mortar shells start raining down.

All calibers, all kinds, all over the place. Someone has

decided to annihilate everything in the area, assuming that if everything is wiped out we'll be wiped out too.

I shove the general against the rock face under an over-hang and push my revolver into his stomach.

What is it you have on the general of the Northern Command? Let's have it, and fast.

I'm not talking to you.

Liora, I say. Pull his pants down.

Without looking at anyone Liora walks over to the general, undoes his belt, and slides his pants down to his ankles.

Now his shorts.

No, says the general. I'll talk.

Take his shorts down anyway, Liora. I want to see his dick while he's talking.

Liora pulls his shorts down.

Now then.

This is very unpleasant.

And killing children isn't?

I haven't killed any.

We all have, including you. Now talk.

He starts talking.

The first time was twenty years ago. A small detachment received orders to make a raid into Syria. I was in command of a company, he was in charge of the whole operation. The Syrians ambushed us. Some were killed, others wounded. We were taken prisoner.

They wanted to know who the commander was. He told them it was him. And who was the second-in-command. That was me. They told us to talk. We refused. They brought in one of the wounded and slaughtered him right in front of us. When they were about to slaughter another one, he started talking. I did too. Then they killed all the prisoners except the two of us who had talked—we were the only ones left alive. Later there was a prisoner exchange. Both of us returned as heroes. The Syrians didn't mind sending us back, we had told them all they needed to know. After that, he soared through the ranks like a rocket. And so did I. Don't think he isn't a good soldier. He's an exceptional soldier. Anyone would have talked in that situation. You can be a hero when they're about to slaughter you but not when they're slaughtering your buddy. We spilled everything, names, places, details. Before they let us go, they brought in a whole company of animals and both of us were gang-raped. War isn't always fun, you know.

Go on, I say.

Well, at least I didn't cash in on it. But he went on to have himself interviewed by the media, to tell them what a great hero he had been.

Well, that was sweet, I say. What about the second time?

The second time it was the other way around. We had caught a bunch of terrorists who had infiltrated on a sabotage mission. By then, both of us were fairly high-ranking officers. After we killed the first one, the four others talked. After they talked, we killed them all. You won't find me feeling sorry for those bastards who come here to kill children. But it was a violation of orders from the general staff, and that could have meant a court-martial with at best a reprimand, a temporary demotion, and a blot on our records.

Tell me the name of the wounded man those Syrians slaughtered.

He tells me a name. I pick up the radio.

This is Free Ein Harod, over.

This is the general of the Northern Command, over.

General, I am going to give you a name. You'll understand what it's about.

I have nothing to say to you. You are dead.

Wrong, General. Listen, General, what does the name Isaac Naim mean to you?

A brief silence. Then:

What do you want?

Stop firing. Evacuate all forces from here. Give me an

armored car with a driver, and ride with us as far as Megiddo.

Or else?

Or else I start singing on the radio. And someone is going to hear me sing. Because I have another little song that's interesting too, and as you know, headquarters listens in on all frequencies.

Give me five minutes.

Ten seconds is what you have. One, two, three, four, five, six.

Stop. It's a deal. Now let me tell you something. Your children are alive.

I know.

How do you know that, you bastard?

Because I am like you, General, just like you.

Now listen, Ein Harod, the children are going to stay here, and whatever happens to me will happen to them.

General, bring some blankets, some food, and a bottle of scotch.

Scotch? What for?

I'd like to drink your health.

How about some Chivas?

Chivas is fine, over.

The artillery fire dies down. Only when you know the sounds of war can you really appreciate the silence when they stop.

I see it coming. With clenched fists Liora throws herself at me and starts pummeling my face.

Assassin, she yells, you're all assassins, and you're an assassin just like all the others!

I don't even try to protect myself. She beats me until she gets tired and sinks to the ground, sobbing. I take the radio.

Pick a place to wait for me with the armored car and the driver and the rest of it.

Tell me your present location.

No need. I have an excellent guide, a brigadier general. Give me the coordinates.

He gives them to me. Then he goes on to say, I'm an army general, I am armed, and I'll stay armed. If that doesn't suit you, don't come. The driver will be unarmed, over.

I tell Mahmoud to straighten out the general's clothing. We have to be on our way. But where?

Not to the coordinates the general has given us, that's for sure. Someone who has decided to kill us all isn't going to give up easily. His coordinates are a deathtrap. We have to go somewhere else, and fast. But where is that?

There's only one place.

Take us to Ein Harod, I tell Rafi.

We start walking. He knows the terrain like the palm of his hand. Moving only in the folds of the land, we never cross open spaces.

How long would it take us to get to that meeting point from here?

Not long, says Rafi, maybe an hour.

Well, now I know. We have less than an hour to escape death.

The radio is out—I didn't remember to ask for batteries. The military radio only receives a certain wavelength. I have no idea what is going on in Ein Harod, just as I had no way of knowing whether what I'd heard on the radio, when I had a radio, was really true. And all I have is less than an hour, and I have to think, and I have to think alone because I am alone.

Who are you, Liora? Who are you, Liora of Ein Harod?

They don't tell me anything, she said. Perhaps it's because my parents are there. I left the kibbutz some time ago. Don't ask me, it hurts, she said. But I have to know. I have to know every mountain, every valley, every tree, every house, and every woman on the road to Ein Harod. Because he who does not know the road that is neither short nor long will never get there.

Has Ein Harod fallen? In every fallen fortress there is an old woman who does not want to die, and sometimes also a young woman who wants to live.

Well, I've had my moment with her, a moment under the starry sky. Let's get out of here, she said, I'll take you to Ein Harod. So maybe Ein Harod has not fallen. But if it hasn't, why isn't she there, in Ein Harod? What is she doing here? But, I know, in every fortress there is one who slips out in the dead of night and joins the enemy. A prophet who knows, a sage who has understood, or just someone who wants to save his skin. Had she escaped from a siege by slipping away at night, without a sound? Did her old lover, General Rafi, wait for her? Or was he the officer in charge of the besieging forces, and had his soldiers presented him with this fugitive from Ein Harod?

Had he taken pity on the beautiful refugee and, with a wave of the victor's scepter, granted her her life? Had the way of all flesh then joined them together? But she said that she owed him nothing. No, Liora, I don't know who you are. All I know is that you, Liora, believe that Ein Harod may not have fallen yet. At least not up to the time I took Rafi prisoner. Let's go to Ein Harod, she said.

We walk quickly, my head bursting with thoughts while my body pushes itself to the utmost in order to arrive, at any cost, at the place beyond which there is no longer any need for hope.

Why have they laid waste to Ein Hahoresh? "We'll raise the red flag high": that's what we sang at Ein Hahoresh. Maybe Ein Hahoresh was brought down from within, maybe it laid waste to itself. Woe to him who has ever raised a flag on high. But has Ein Harod too been crushed in the meantime, perhaps also from within? And what about me? Where am I going, if not to raise a flag in Ein Harod?

Mahmoud is marching along, deep in thought. And who are you, Mahmoud? To what end will we arrive together at the place where we must part? Once, perhaps twice, he has saved my life, and now I don't know whether I am his salvation or whether I am Death who appeared before him at an orchard's edge.

And how beautiful the world is at this moment, even while you are abandoning it.

Ein Harod is on Mahmoud's way. On his way where?

Even when you're fleeing, your eyes notice everything. Now and again we cross an old building site. The stones of the terrace are covered by lichen. Lichen is a symbiosis: algae and fungi feeding on each other. Each gives the other what it has and takes what it does not have.

And what would happen if they decided to declare the ultimate war for possession of the single stone on which they both live?

Only the stone would remain, bare.

The things you think of on the run.

That general of the Northern Command, the tough guy. Crazy as well—there was a smell of his craziness in the air. Why did he send Liora into the cave? Was it to tell Rafi, May your final hours be sweet? Had she realized why she had been sent and then decided to say what she'd said and not what she hadn't? Why didn't Rafi get the message right away? Maybe he isn't as bright as all that. And I know that love can be a killer.

And how lovely the world is at this moment, and why have I not stopped running away from it?

No, I won't let all this happen ever again. Me, I'm going to Ein Harod, and we'll start over from the very beginning, but this time everything will be different. There, in the new Ein Harod, the lion will lie down with the lamb, the earth will be reborn and yield its fruits anew.

Ein Harod, Mahmoud suddenly says. He's not taking us there the right way.

Of course I am, says Rafi. I'm going to Ein Harod.

Maybe you're going, says Mahmoud, but you won't get there.

Why not? I ask.

Because this way is too short.

What do you suggest? asks Rafi.

That we go in the opposite direction, says Mahmoud.

Of course he's right. It comes to me in a flash. Anything that might occur to Rafi or me will also occur to the general of the Northern Command. He'll be waiting for us at precisely the spot where we think to evade him. All of us come from the same godforsaken hole.

Mahmoud, however, is from another village. He may well be the only one who knows the third road, the one that is neither short nor long. Something like Carthage to Ein Harod via the Alps.

We double back. Lose contact with the enemy. Hide. Start moving again in a very large circle. Preferably to the east. Not via Megiddo. Megiddo, that's Armageddon, our killing field.

He takes us southeast. Like Rafi, he knows how to find dead terrain. He makes us march at least ten kilometers to make sure that we're out of range of those who are hunting for our souls. By then we have to be in a shelter that can't be detected even from the air. No doubt the moment will come when they realize we've tricked them, and then they'll mobilize all available forces and make an all-out effort.

After five or ten minutes Rafi suddenly says, Mahmoud is right, but we won't make it walking. We have to run for it.

I know what he's saying. About fifty minutes from now they'll start getting nervous. An hour from now they'll start weighing all the possibilities and make plans. An hour and a half from now, all available forces will be at every likely spot, and two hours from now we'll be stone-cold dead. Unless we've covered twenty—no, twenty-five kilometers in those two hours.

I remember how Enoch ran from Ein Ghedi to Kalia in two hours back in 1942 to get help after a grenade had exploded near the campfire, and nine of us never came back from that desert march. Enoch Longlegs, now pushing up daisies in Beth Alfa. And I remember forced marches of forty kilometers, even sixty, in the mountains. Still, that's nothing compared to the Japanese and their eighty kilometers in twenty-four hours with a full pack. If we aren't Japanese now, we may not get there.

So we start running. Rafi first, setting the pace. Mahmoud doesn't have to tell him which direction, he knows.

Rafi is a magnificent runner. He reminds me of the running of Ahimaaz. But Mahmoud, too, is moving along as if he'd been doing it all his life.

Liora runs like a gazelle. I just run, bringing up the rear. The wind is making her shirt flutter, and I am running, short of breath, thirty-five years older than I was on my last expedition, with tarred lungs, muscles long gone, and she is running in front of me, showing a curve here, a rounded spot there, and suddenly I feel young in my pants and want her very much, so much that I don't want to leave her, to lose her, and so I keep running.

Rafi is setting exactly the right pace. From time to time he looks back, merely to check, or so it seems to me, if I'm still there. I'm a little embarrassed. Well, whatever. I'm beginning to hope that we'll get there after all, one way or the other. God, listen to my prayer and by your grace make me cross these mountains just this one time.

Run. Run fast. Run faster.

A last smile, *au revoir*. I had stayed home to work, my wife had gone to celebrate with her friends. Just a smile at the door, just a simple parting.

We have reached the foothills of the range that descends to the valley of Hefer. From here we can see a landscape of plains and woods and orchards, pastures and swamps. Mahmoud picks up speed and passes Rafi. Now I see where we are.

The wild pigs' lair.

Once a pig, always a pig. I know very well that even before

spending the night in their lair, I was already their brother and comrade.

Then we hear them.

It's the voice of the general of the Northern Command coming over a loudspeaker. Don't move, he says. You are surrounded and covered.

All of us drop to the ground, but that's no use.

Get up, slowly, with your hands up high.

Get up, says Rafi, it's all over. We're fucked.

We get up.

Keep walking the way you were. But without guns. We can see you. Throw down your weapons or we'll shoot you on the spot.

We do as we're told and start walking. Then we see them. It's a shallow depression, just big enough for two helicopters and one armored car. Close to the car stands the general of the Northern Command, holding a submachine gun. I'm sure it's him, just as I'm sure that all the paratroopers from the helicopters have already taken up their positions and are covering us.

Come on, says the general. Let's see you close up.

We walk over.

Welcome to Samarkand, says the general with a smile.

He's a hefty fellow, almost a giant. His face is not overly tough, but it isn't amiable either. He smiles at me and says, You know the story about Samarkand?

Yes, I say. I know quite a few stories.

And you know the prayer "Let there be no hope for traitors"?

"Praised be the Judge of the Ultimate Truth."

Amen, says the general, amen selah. You see, busy as I am, responsible to the state and all, I still find the time to personally settle my little accounts with an assortment of shitheads and assholes. Look at this piece of crap here. Can you believe that used to be a man? Yet if I hadn't talked at the time, he would have had us all slaughtered without a word.

Until now, he hasn't even looked at Rafi. He's taking his time, he's in no hurry.

You know you are a certifiable nutcase, says Rafi. And you'll be hauled in front of a court-martial. I want to talk to the chief of staff immediately.

He's sleeping at the moment, says the general. We can't wake him up. And you don't have anyone by the balls anymore. All you're holding now is shit, just raise your hand to your nose and smell it. And by the way, I see that you've been using the brain of the Arabush to try to get the hell out. They're great at that. This must be the Arabush?

Absolutely right, Your Excellency.

And by the way, he says, I imagine you understand that you're all under arrest.

And by the way, I say, where's the scotch?

Rafi, says the general, get the whiskey. Rafi the driver himself gets out of the armored car. He is holding a bottle. He hands it to the general and gets back behind the wheel. The general opens the bottle and hands it to me.

To your short life, he says.

How short, General?

As short as from here to Ein Harod. And do you know what? I really am taking you to Ein Harod, all four of you.

To your life, General, I say, and take a long swig. You have any children, General?

Yes, God be praised, three. Great kids.

To the lives of your children, General.

To the lives of yours, Free Ein Harod. By the way, you haven't toasted Ein Harod yet.

Right. Here's to Free Ein Harod.

I drink. A few seconds short of eternity I let go of the bottle. Drink, I tell Mahmoud.

I'm a Moslem.

So drink like a man who doesn't drink.

Mahmoud has a drink like a man who doesn't drink.

The general picks up his radio and speaks. A company of paratroopers bursts on the scene.

Tie them up, all of them, says the general. They tie us up, hands behind our backs, ankles hobbled.

Should we blindfold them? asks the commanding officer.

Don't bother. Ours is a beautiful country, let them see it.

They make us get in the armored car. The general gets in next to the driver. We are in the back with four armed paras. So here we are, shit, let's go.

And by the way, Ex–Brigadier General, the general says without turning around, maybe you'd like to know why you can't get through to the chief of staff or to the prime minister either. Let me tell you why. Now it can be told: the chief of staff, that's me. Someone has to save the country from all these morons, right?

Rafi starts frothing at the mouth. Then his head slumps back.

You don't have to have any particular temperament to fall into a state of shock. I had already seen tough, courageous, and clearheaded men like Rafi fall victim to shock in combat. I would probably be in the same shape he's in if I hadn't known all along, from the moment those men came to kill me, that there was no hope for me anyway.

Speaking of that, I say, where is the former chief of staff?

Oh, with all the others. With his prime minister and all the other ministers. In three weeks they managed to fuck everything up. Now they're pushing up daisies in Ein Harod.

Liora bursts into tears.

Don't cry, my beauty, the general says reassuringly, we don't execute whores. By the way, perhaps one of you can recommend a good prime minister to me? The kind who is a cut above everybody and knows how to lead this unfortunate people—under my wing, naturally. Yes, a cut above everybody except for me.

How about Mahmoud? I suggest.

I don't think so, says the general, not cracking a smile. He ain't right. And besides, all these Arabushes, we're really fucking their mothers now, in the ass. I don't think we can go for a prime minister whose mother we're fucking at the same time.

I sure wouldn't want to fuck your mother, says Mahmoud.

By the way, says the general, would someone back there be kind enough to hit the Arabush over the head with a gun butt? Don't worry about cracking his skull. And by the way, where were we?

The officer sitting next to me hits Mahmoud on the head. Mahmoud doesn't pass out. Groaning, he slumps to the floor of the car, his face covered with blood.

We were discussing a guide for this unfortunate people, I say. And in your shoes I'd be insulted if an Arabush wouldn't fuck my mother.

What would you do to him?

I'd order him to fuck my mother.

Good idea, says the general. By the way, would someone back there be kind enough to hit the dirty little Jew on the head?

I get mine. I don't pass out either. I just crumple, blood on my face, thinking that the general really likes the expression "by the way." By the way, I ask him a few minutes later, where are you taking us?

Untie his hands, the general says, so he can get up and see where he's going. And by the way, that's a dumb question. We're going to Ein Harod, where else?

They untie my hands, help me to my feet. I take my handkerchief and wipe the blood off my forehead and out of my eyes. Now I can see.

O Eretz Israel, my beauty, Zion, my well-beloved, my delight. For a moment I'm oblivious to everything—Ein Harod, all the deaths I have seen, this horror that is my life and that now runs to its final shore in this enchanted azure.

I am standing, leaning against the side of the car. Olive

groves, stone terraces, oaks, sacred tombs, altars to Baal and shrines to Ashtoreth, rivers flowing with water in winter and blood in summer, battlefields and sites of massacres, black goats on the mountainside, vines twining around houses, a braying donkey, rebels dead in caves, crucified ones along the roads, cypresses touching the stars at night, and the God of armies, most terrible of all gods, this is His kingdom at the foot of Mount Megiddo, Armageddon.

This is the time to believe in God, says the general, breaking into my thoughts without turning his head. Now or never. Do you want to know why this is the time? Let me tell you. Because soon you'll be drooling for a simple little bullet in the head like in the good old days. Then it'll be too late. Look what a beautiful country you're about to lose.

I don't say anything.

Tell me, Mr. Free Ein Harod, you've never toyed with the idea of becoming prime minister?

Certainly not now, I say. Maybe after you, once all of you are gone.

See, he says to me, I knew it, you're one of us. You think exactly the way we do. About what it'll be like when all the others are gone. So what difference is there between us?

I know I don't have an answer to that. Even if I did, what use would it be? Once I thought I knew, but today isn't once.

You know, the general says to me, I know all about you. I've read your dossier. Fantastic. Quite a killer when you had to be. If I could be sure you'd be a good thief too, I might make you prime minister after all. As a matter of fact, I sort of almost like you.

I don't like his liking me. But what can I say to him about all that? That I have at least one consolation: I did not seek him out—his people came to my house to kill me, to my own door. I still don't like it. Who knows, if they hadn't come to kill me, if they hadn't taken my kids hostage, maybe I would have just killed myself without further ado. Who knows if it wouldn't have been better to just let them wipe me out.

Suddenly, confronted with the general of the Northern Command, who has taken me prisoner and now says he likes me, I feel a terrible weariness.

Tell me something, says the general. In my place, in Syria, would you have kept your mouth shut and died?

I don't know.

Don't lie to me. You do know. Tell me the truth.

I don't want to tell the truth.

All right. I give you permission to lie. Lie to me.

I would have talked. I would have told them everything. But later I would have confessed that I had talked.

See, you even know how to lie. From here to Ein Harod, you're the prime minister.

What was the point of that charade with my kids?

That was just to see how determined you were.

I have nothing to say to that.

Why don't you ask me whether we decided that you were indeed determined?

I've had it with questions, General. Over and out.

Rafi snaps out of his stupor. His head rises, blood returns to his face.

I want a blindfold, he says. I don't want to see what I'm seeing.

Don't worry, you'll get a blindfold when the time comes, says the general. So why don't you take a good look at everything now, see how beautiful the world is, even without you.

Rafi is silent.

But I catch an expression in his eyes that I've seen once or twice in Mahmoud's.

Then I am struck by an appalling thought. I realize that I haven't set eyes on a single Arab all along this road. It gives me the shivers. Village upon village. Everything's green. And the donkey is braying, the sheep grazing, only the people are not there, and if they aren't there, where are they?

I remember the vacant villages greeting us when we conquered the Vaheb. A donkey, a hen, some frightened chicks, an old paralyzed woman, a blind old man.

I remember all those things, think about it all, have all those images rise in front of my eyes, frozen in the glaciers of time. I also see myself as I was then, standing and listening to the barking of abandoned dogs, breathing in the smoke of the abandoned cattle-dung fires rising from still-warm tabouns.

If there were moments of weakness then, they passed. Rage took over again. Grab that rifle.

You don't seem to understand. The general breaks my chain of thought. The good old days are over.

You're right, so they are, I say. Just let me weep alone.

I think about my wife. She would not have gone through with all this. She would have preferred to die. Not because she doesn't love life—she just doesn't want it at any price. If they had come to kill her, she would have been sad, to be sure, sad as those are who love life and make sense of it. Yet she wouldn't have raised a finger against evil, because nothing can be done against it. Whoever decides to fight evil becomes evil himself.

I don't agree with her about that. We have had numerous arguments about the matter. But I can understand her. If that wasn't my particular madness, I would have thrown in the towel long ago. And if it hadn't been for that madness, I now think, I would not have gone out to conquer the Vaheb in those distant days.

I would not have fired at British soldiers in the streets of Jerusalem, in broad daylight and at night. I would not have planted a land mine on the road to Bethlehem. I would not have marched arm in arm with death across a thorny field at Romema that starry night. I would not have disowned my father and my mother and my brothers and sisters, and I would not have made Zion-Jerusalem the focus of my life. For what is this Jerusalem compared to life itself, and what is greater than life and what is less than Zion-Jerusalem when it's a question of conquest or death? So I went and conquered a mountain, and then a valley and another valley, and with my sword I smote to the left and to the right to dispossess the Canaanite and the Hittite and the Jebusite and the Guirgashite, and I felt no pity for Amalek, or compassion for Edom or the sons of Ketura. Like a lightning bolt I struck into their midst and marched onward, marching and striking, striking and weeping, ever onward, and did not stop until Vaheb had been smitten and conquered and the storm had passed, gone as if it had never happened, and I alone remained, empty and hollow like Chekhov's revolver at the end of the last act.

In 1947 I was a student at Mount Skopos University. Saturdays I would go down to Tel Aviv, and Sunday mornings I would return to Jerusalem to pursue my studies. On the way into the city there was a lunatic asylum. As we passed it we heard a long, horrifying shout, a shout of only one syllable but multiplied by the echo from the surrounding mountains.

Once I rode on the bus with Uriella. She was a psychology student at the university. She told me that a very long time ago that single syllable had been a long speech—organized and reasoned. In the course of the years that speech had shrunk to its most elementary significance, this shout of all shouts. The unfortunate madman, imprisoned there for the rest of his days, would die with a whisper, because even his shout would be silenced. But once upon a time he had had something to say.

Jesus himself on the cross, I'm sure of it, had he lived long enough hanging from his nails, would have forgotten those seven last words of his. They would have turned into a shout, his shout fading to a whisper, and when there was nothing to even whisper anymore he would have died, at last. And now I'm wondering if I haven't reached my own whispering stage.

Shout! I yell at Mahmoud. Shout something to wake me up—because I'm afraid that I won't!

I believe he's going to do it. He gets up off the floor of the car, his face still covered with blood. His chest expands, his neck veins swell, but he does not shout. Perhaps he still has something to say before it all turns into a shout.

Stop the car for a moment, he says. I want to sing.

Stop, I tell the general. I want to hear Mahmoud sing.

Stop, says the general. Free Ein Harod wants to hear the Arabush sing.

The driver stops the car. Mahmoud gets out, hands and legs tied, sinks to his knees, and touches his forehead to the ground. Then he raises his head again.

O my land, my homeland, he sings out. O land, my land.

It is a modulated chant, a lament, and it makes me shiver.

O land, my land, Mahmoud chants. And I know that when he sings of his land, which is my land, he is singing of his land, which is not mine. And he kneels upright like a blind man and sings, and the same terrible sadness overwhelms me as on the day I turned and saw my home for the last time. That was one of those days when you leave for the wars one more time, not knowing whether you'll return.

I look at the land. In Mahmoud's land I do not exist. He is not singing about the tombs of my ancestors. My land, he sings, but I have never been part of it. In Mahmoud's land I have neither parcel nor patrimony.

He is not singing about my rebels or my martyrs or my crucified or decapitated ones. On this land no tears have been shed by my prophets, Jeremiah of Anatoth has not lamented, "Oh mother of mine, why did you give me life?" and Amos, who dwelled among the shepherds at Tekoa, has not prophesied the three crimes of Israel. My distant ancestor has not carved in stone the names of the year's twelve months, the month of Bul, the month of Etanim. My forebears have not built and carved out the terraces on the mountains' flanks, nor have they sat down each one at peace

under his vine, each under his fig tree, they have not carried
the first fruits of their soil to the temple of the supreme God,
creator of Heaven and Earth.

Vaheb is not, nor did that storm occur. At Ein Gedi,
Shulamith was not, nor has the Preacher of Ecclesiastes
said, "All is vanity," nor have my forefathers gone out in the
morning to their vineyards to see if the vine has flowered
and the pomegranate ripened.

My last king was not crucified at Antioch, his hands and
feet were not cut off, nor his head taken by the sword. My
land, Mahmoud is singing, but in his land I have neither part
nor parcel, in his land I have no patrimony.

A wispy cloud appears on the horizon.

A flight of starlings or other migrants, because it is
always at this time, in this season, that they pass by here, on
the road that leads from the end of summer to the beginning
of spring—which may seem backward, but it really is the
true road. Am I not, too, starling and wild duck, stork and
crane, am I not returning to spring in Ein Harod by the
inverted route that is the true way, the road neither short
nor long?

Bravo, the general says to Mahmoud. You could have been
a great singer.

If you ask me, I would have shot him, says Rafi. Right
here, on his land.

And what would that have done for you?

One less.

I have nothing to say to that. Mahmoud gets back into the
armored car. We're on our way again.

Listen, you, you won't be shooting anyone anymore, not
even an Arabush, says the general of the Northern Command. As a matter of fact, not only will you never shoot
anyone again, but you'll be shot yourself. We'll soon be there,
and then it's the court-martial, the death sentence for deser-
tion and treason, the firing squad. You know the procedure.

Rafi—Rafi the driver, that is—stomps on the brakes and

whips out a revolver. I assume the general has been antici-
pating this, simply waiting for it to happen. At the very
moment Rafi brakes, the general slams him over the head
with the butt of his automatic.

Take him, he says to the paratroop officer, and tie him up
tighter than the others. I knew he was going to try that. He's
a faithful one. Hats off to that. He'll go up against the wall
with his boss. "Dearly beloved in life, neither in death were
they parted."

The paras drag Rafi the driver out and tie him up. Then
they deposit him on the floor of the car. The officer takes the
wheel. That poor asshole, says Rafi the general. I knew it.

Why didn't you warn him?

It wouldn't have made any difference. That scumbag gave
him the wheel deliberately.

We are on our way again.

Tell us now, Rafi, before they shoot you, what really happened in Ein Harod.

They're not going to shoot me.

Who's not going to shoot you?

That pinhead isn't. He's the chief of staff like you're the
prime minister. Don't tell me you believe that bullshit.

Rafi, that pinhead is not a dream. This is what's happening. Wake up. Come on, tell me what went on at Ein Harod,
because later it will be too late, seeing as you'll be dead by
tonight.

Not tonight, says the general. Tomorrow morning. At
dawn. In a field. I hope the weather is nice. Such a handsome
man deserves to die on a fine spring morning.

General, says Liora, if it wouldn't be too complicated, I
want to die tomorrow morning too.

Out of the question. I told you who we *don't* execute.

Liora blushes. No kidding—in this armored car lumber-
ing up a steep, dusty road, she is blushing.

From those roseate cheeks I gather you get the message,
sweetheart. You know, I'm not one of those types who like

them dead. I like a moist cunt, trembling with desire, sweetness, and tenderness. You get what I'm saying?

We don't talk like that to women, says Mahmoud.

What do you need a woman for, Arabush? Take a goat. One more peep out of you and you'll get it again. By the way, would someone back there be so kind as to give him a crack on the head, a good one?

They hit him again.

I am seized by a strange, sudden weakness. I throw up. Mahmoud lies on the floor of the car covered with vomit and blood. I throw up again.

With trembling fingers I take out a cigarette and light it.

Once there was a happy summer, a summer without bloodshed. There is such a thing, a summer with no bloodshed. Once every who knows how many years, once in a few generations, we have a summer without bloodshed.

We had gone to the vineyard, Mahmoud's vineyard. Not this Mahmoud, another Mahmoud, in another era.

Someone had brought a guitar, someone else an oud. We were lying on our backs under the vines, with grapes hanging above our heads. We had brought some bottles of arrack. We made coffee. We sang songs and played games, laughed and talked, and for a moment the country belonged to all of us. For a moment Mahmoud's village was a homeland for me, for a moment Tel Aviv was a homeland for Mahmoud.

Then that summer was over, and it was the one, unique, and last summer without bloodshed. So much for that.

Why don't you ask me where the Arabs are? the general prompts me.

Where are they?

They are no longer. We sent them away.

Where?

To Mecca. Where they came from. Now they can ride camels in the sand and sing their songs.

I say nothing.

When we get there we'll wipe out these two sons of

whores, and then we'll send your Arabush back to Mecca to join the others. He can sing his ditties as much as he wants there.

No response from me.

Why don't you ask me what we're going to do with the villages?

What are you going to do with them?

Now then, we have a plan. We are going to run the bull-dozers all over here, and in a couple of months at the most, there won't even be a trace left.

Like Ein Hahoresh? I ask. Or perhaps like Ein Harod?

Like everywhere, the general replies, like everywhere. And now I'm going to sing you a little song. I'm sure you've heard it before. "No more tradition's chains shall bind us, arise ye slaves, no more in thrall. The earth shall rise on new foundations, we have been nought, we shall be all."

You could've been a great singer, I say.

By the way, says the general, you've probably noticed that even though you can't see a single Arab around, here and there you can see a donkey or a herd of goats. Let me tell you why that's so. With those donkeys we had a moral problem. On the one hand, is it the donkey's fault that its master is an Arab? On the other, both donkey and goat are descendants of the donkeys and goats of our ancestors who lived here, so they have a right to live here, right?

No smiles, no chuckles. No birdsong, no braying of don-keys.

Mahmoud tries to get up. One of the paratroopers helps him. My hands are free, and I ask the para for a rag. He opens a satchel and hands me a yellow cleaning cloth. I wipe the blood and vomit off Mahmoud's face and neck. It makes me gag once again, but it seems I don't have anything left to throw up.

Without knowing exactly why, I also wipe the blood off Rafi the driver's face. Up to now, no one has paid any atten-tion to him. Not even his superior officer, with whom he'll be executed tomorrow morning. I tell myself, Today I clean and fix up those who are going to die. There shouldn't be any old blood on the faces of those whose fresh blood will be spilled for the last time.

The general's radio starts crackling.

Everybody out! Take these assholes to some tree and leave them there. I want to be by myself.

We are taken out and laid down at the foot of a big tree. The paratroop officer hands me a cigarette, hands one to Rafi the general as well. From here we can't hear who the general is talking to or about what.

I pull a cigarette out of my pocket, set it between Mahmoud's lips, and light it for him. He says nothing. His gaze is clouded but not vacant, the gaze of a man lost in terrible thoughts.

You don't happen to have a newspaper? I ask the officer. Any paper would do.

What do you need a paper for? And you surprise me. Surely you know there aren't any newspapers anymore?

Why not?

There just aren't any. I don't know. Who needs them?

Well, they'd tell us what's happening in Japan.

Let the Japanese worry about what goes on there.

I have nothing to say to that, so I don't reply.

Listen, Rafi says to the officer, you don't look stupid.

I've heard that before.

If you've heard it, you better believe it.

If I believed you, I'd be stupid all right.

Sometimes it's worth it to be stupid, I tell the officer. Just untie us, no noise.

I'm not sure that's the right thing to do, says the officer.

So you're loyal.

Yes, I am. To my homeland.

There's only one of those, says Rafi.

Damn straight, says the officer.

Tell me, is he really chief of staff now?

Presently, yes.

And what does the homeland say about that?

It isn't speaking to me directly. Only through proper channels.

What is your conscience telling you?

No comment, the officer says. But at the corner of his mouth I notice that tremor of the divided soul, of mixed emotions, characteristic of a suffering conscience. I give him an understanding smile.

We hear the horn of the armored car. The general waves his arm. End of intermission. We're taken back to the car, the journey continues. We're no longer on a dirt road but back on the paved highway.

Rafi, says the general, perhaps you'd like to know what I just heard?

Someone's broken the law and killed a donkey?

Wrong, the general says. Let me tell you. Your division tried to rebel, but the mutiny has been put down. You'll soon see your three colonels in the stockade. They'll be shot too. And by the way, have you any idea how they knew you'd been taken prisoner?

Someone ought to kill you, I say.

Maybe so, but who?

Maybe me, I say.

The general thinks that one over for a few seconds. Then he says, Yes, maybe you. But that would be it for your kids as well.

I know, I tell him.

I can see the Megiddo police station looming up. Armageddon, the last stop on the road to Ein Harod.

I check my watch. It's almost five in the afternoon. The gates swing open, our armored car drives in and comes to a stop in the yard. The side doors are opened, and we step down one by one. A group of policemen is standing guard. The general speaks to their corporal in a low voice. Two military policemen take hold of each one of us and march us

off. The general waves absentmindedly. He looks preoc-
cupied.

I'm familiar with prisons and don't feel displaced, afraid,
or even lonely after they've deposited me in the cell, with its
single barred window opening onto the inner courtyard,
and the steel door has slammed shut behind me. I pick a
corner and sit down on the floor, my back to the wall. They'll
come when they're ready.

This is one of the fortresses built by the British in 1936.
High-grade concrete, extremely thick walls. After the British departed, all these buildings became police stations or
prisons. I remember doing time in five of them at different
points in my life. My cell gives me a feeling of déjà vu. So
many steps from one wall to the other during the long hours;
fifteen minutes of exercise in the morning, another fifteen at
night; the bucket in the corner; always visible to the guard
through the peephole in the door.

Well, we've certainly been separated now. In twelve
hours Rafi will be executed. For me, Liora, Mahmoud,
what remains is simply a matter of patience and waiting
rooms, as Gazi would say, the man who once promised me
that the sun would rise in the west one day. Surely he
meant that tomorrow's sun would rise on tomorrow's world.
For Rafi, the sun would not rise at all tomorrow, not even in
the east.

I have no idea how long I stayed there, hunkered down on
the concrete, my back against the wall. Probably hours. In
the end I must have allowed myself to fall asleep.

I wake up covered with cold sweat and trembling all over.
I don't know what has jerked me out of sleep. Oh, but I do.
The smell of death is in the air. The smell that fills animals
led to the slaughterhouse with fear and helplessness. It is
what wakes the prisoners up at dawn on the day of an
execution in the prison yard. No one needs to tell them. No
one needs to tell me either.

It is still dark, but there is a pale gray streak on the

eastern horizon. And the gazelle of dawn, pale-fingered Eos, outshines the waxing moon.

Three stakes have been set up in the yard. Rafi, division commander, has been tied to the one in the middle, a black blindfold across his eyes. To his right, Rafi the driver, to his left, Mahmoud. They too have been blindfolded. In front of them all, the firing squad.

I don't have time to ask myself why Mahmoud too. There's a burst of gunfire. The three slump slowly, their fall slowed by their hands tied behind the poles.

I am sure that Liora too is watching.

I look around for the general of the Northern Command. He isn't there.

I turn away and throw myself on the concrete floor. I try to cry, but the tears won't come. A huge bloodstain envelops my consciousness. I fall asleep.

At seven in the morning I'm awakened by shouts. Breakfast. Two military policemen come in, one carrying a tray, the other covering me with his submachine gun. They leave, the door closes behind them.

I eat. I take a shit. I feel like thinking about something but can't manage it. I want to think, Why Mahmoud? No go. I want to think about what is going to happen, to me, to Liora, but don't get anywhere with that either.

So I pace in my cell, from wall to wall, for hours. At noon they come back with lunch. The food is edible, I have no complaints. I take a nap. No one bothers me. I wake up again in the late afternoon. I start pacing around the cell again. No visitors. No interrogations. In the evening the door opens one more time: dinner. The food is edible. No complaints.

I sit down in the corner, back to the wall. No image appears before my eyes. No memories.

But I can think.

Mahmoud shouldn't have died.

There are things we should have said to one another. Maybe I should have gotten out of the armored car and stood in that field with him and sung my own song. Maybe we should have paid close attention to see if it wasn't the same song after all and if it really wouldn't be possible to sing it together.

And he shouldn't have died in a war that may well not have been his. There are enough people who get themselves killed in wars they believe are theirs. Mahmoud had no citizen's rights and should not have been killed as if he were a citizen.

And Mahmoud's life story was not meant to end this way. I feel a bitter sensation of guilt, of lack of respect. For Mahmoud too had somewhere to go, just as I do. And he had almost taken me to Ein Harod, but I had not taken him where he wanted to go.

I never tried to find out where he wanted to go. Yet when we took to the road together, I had Ein Harod in mind and he had something else, and he never told me what that something was. Apart from a few necessary exchanges we said nothing to each other, and now it was too late.

As for me, I imagined that once I got to Ein Harod everything would start over from the beginning and in a new way. You see, I did believe that Ein Harod was what would remain while all the rest of it disappeared—because otherwise there was no way to go on, there just wasn't. Now that Mahmoud is gone, to whom can I pass the message of Ein Harod, to whom can I say, Come see me in Ein Harod, whoever you are, come see me in Ein Harod, no matter where you come from?

I won't forgive them Mahmoud's senseless and meaningless death. If it's the last thing I do, I'll take bloody revenge for Mahmoud. I don't see myself as the hand of destiny or its sword, I won't do it because of a code of honor or because of war, friendship, or love: we weren't friends or comrades. But we were brothers, brothers in something that we had not had time to grasp, and now it is too late. If I am condemned to avenge Mahmoud's blood, it is for a single reason: if I don't do it, I won't get to Ein Harod. And that is why I am a sword now.

I feel overcome with weariness and stretch out on the floor.

Time to lose your mind.

I am in a cave in Galilee. Around me there are corpses. I am the only survivor. With my companions I have fled here from the Romans, but this has been our last stand.

Ben-Matitiahou! Joseph Ben-Matitiahou! Come out of the cave! Come out with your hands up! You hear me, Ben-Matitiahou. Come out with your hands in the air!

I come out of the cave, my hands up. The general is standing in front of me, even more gigantic than before. I'm just a little grasshopper at his feet. He is wearing a laurel wreath. He looks down at me with an expression that blends contempt and pity, envy and hatred, and disgust as well.

Go, he says, and don't look back. Only if you go forward and don't look back, only then will you reach Ein Harod.

I wake up with a start. I must not have heard them banging on the door, because they never come into a sleeping prisoner's cell without waking him up first, but there they are, uninvited hosts in a dream that isn't theirs.

The general looks at me with a smile. This is no time to sleep, he says. All this time you've been jabbering Ein Harod, Ein Harod, and all of a sudden you just fall asleep. Get up, you're coming with me.

I get up. I don't ask where we're going.

You won't believe this, the general says, but these morons have staged a counterrevolution.

What morons?

The three colonels of the general's division. They managed to get away and get the troops behind them.

Who won?

The morons, obviously. And by the way, if you want to know who the bad guys are and who the good guys are, don't bother. We haven't had any good guys for a long time.

What about you?

I'm still alive. And I have one more little thing to take care of in my life. You'll see in a little while.

He has two armed MPs behind him, and yet that son of a whore still carries his submachine gun, shouldering it with the nonchalance of habit that makes it an extension of his body, something he can move like an arm or a leg.

To my surprise, one of the cops pulls a paper handkerchief scented with cologne out of his shirt pocket and wipes my forehead, my face, my neck. They want me to look good, I tell myself in my dream, fresh and perfumed. For the stake, probably.

One MP in front, me in the middle, another MP and the general bringing up the rear, and off we go. The steel door slams shut behind us. I'm not handed my personal belongings, whatever that may mean. We walk down hallways that are familiar from another life. If there is a counterrevolution, it hasn't reached here yet, it's still on its way. And here is the gate to the outside.

Next to the gate, Liora between two policemen. She throws herself into my arms. If we've had a bad moment, that's over now. They have a hard time pulling us apart.

The gate swings open and there's a special limousine, incredibly long, I've seen it at the movies, it's a bulletproof presidential car. The two MPs guarding Liora stay behind. The rest of us get into the car, Liora and me in the back hemmed in by two MPs, the general in front next to a helmeted driver. Not Rafi, to be sure.

We don't drive far. Maybe five hundred meters. It is ten o'clock at night. The hour of coups d'état. I have hardly slept at all.

Barbed wire. A sentry. A gate.

Weird as it seems, I try to figure out the make of the car we're in. I finally decide it is a Mercedes.

The gate opens. A dirt road climbs a small hill whose surface seems strangely brittle. The beams of the headlights carry a long way. We stop, get out.

The general orders the driver and the two MPs to return to the barracks. The three of us go on alone.

There is no building on the hill, not even a road. We walk along on a barely flattened dirt path that you can't even see from a distance. It hasn't been used much—there aren't any footprints. In the road is a sort of manhole covered with a cast-iron lid. The general raises it.

You first, he says to Liora, and you next.

Liora climbs down and I follow. The general switches on his flashlight, and I see a steel ladder against the concrete wall of a shaft, like the entry to a bunker. It is the entry to a bunker. Here we go. The soles of the general's shoes hit my head from time to time. I reach the concrete floor, the general lighting the way. I see a steel door. Keep walking ahead of me, he says.

We get to the door. Next to it there's a fluorescent panel full of pushbuttons. The general punches out a combination, tells me to pull the handle. The door opens. We go in, him last.

A concrete corridor, at the far end another steel door with another fluorescent panel beside it. The general knows the combination. There is a soft hiss, something is approaching. An elevator, no doubt. Here it is, the door opens. We go in, the general pushes a button.

We descend, but not very far. It's not like the ride down in a diamond or gold mine. We stop. Get out. He touches my back with his submachine gun.

Question time:

Why Mahmoud?

Well, there's two versions. The crazy son of a whore tried to kill me. Just as I was going to send him back to Mecca. Right in front of all my men too.

Maybe that was the reason for Mahmoud's clouded look.

The general is still behind me. He could have had a good life in Mecca. But he went for me with a knife. I have no idea where he'd been hiding it.

In his asshole, I suggest. Let's hear the other version. Why Mahmoud?

Why not, that's why. And by the way, it really worked out in terms of symmetry. Jesus with a thief on either side of him. At the end of the corridor we'll turn right.

We turn right. He'll never know which two of the three were the thieves. I could ask him why I am still alive, or why Liora is, but I really don't want to know why—or why not, for that matter.

Yet another door. The general opens it. The light is dazzling.

An enormous room carved out of the rock. I'll be damned. I see where we are now. It's not a bunker, it's another one of those caverns hewn out of rock by my ancestors. The chisel marks on the walls are proof: only the human hand could make those, never a machine.

There are innumerable television screens, video cassette machines, radio sets, telephones, flat maps, relief maps, sandbags, conference tables, armchairs, and so on and so forth.

This is the war command center, he says. The holy of holies.

What war?

Take it easy. All in good time. Now ask me who constructed this place. King Solomon's architect, that's who. Same guy who built Solomon's stables at Megiddo, and the city wall, the gate, and the aqueducts to withstand a siege. But I'm the one who discovered it, and not by accident. I was looking for it. I've always been interested in archeology, and I just knew there had to be an alternative secret defense system underground. The technological and strategic genius who laid out Megiddo had to think of one. And it's a fact.

You've got to admit it, there isn't a better site for it. Just think, for three thousand years this command center has been waiting for the real war. Have a seat.

I sit down. He hasn't spoken to Liora. She remains where she is, standing by the wall.

I see that we are not alone in the command center. There are two armed guards, and their weapons are pointing at me. I know that I have to kill him here, now, tonight. Them's the breaks. All the breaks concerning this place are under his control. True, but time is what I've got, and tonight's the time.

At midnight tonight, says the general, all scores will be settled.

What scores?

All of 'em. You'll see. Stop interrupting me. You see those screens? Each one is a monitor, and each monitor is locked in on a missile, and each missile is locked in on a point in space and a point in time. For instance, the first monitor on the right is aimed at Nineveh, the second on the right at Babylon, and so forth. I'm sure you know that Nineveh and Babylon are archeological sites now, and an archeological site is defined by two coordinates, one in space and one in time.

Now let me tell you something you've never heard before. Any imbecile can think ahead. Any idiot can anticipate the predictable and make it come true. Maybe you were surprised that it was so easy for me to anticipate your moves? Nothing to it. The most pitiful cretin could have foreseen them. Just as any idiot can screw the Arabs. Even a moron like the former chief of staff, may he rest in peace, can seize power. But the one great thing, the truly remarkable thing, is not being able to think ahead: it's the ability to think sideways and back.

All those assholes think they've beaten me now. That's because they can only think ahead. To think ahead means to start out with the givens, add in their consequences, and figure out the right combination. Nothing to it. They have no idea what I've got for them here. Because, you see, I think sideways and back. Tonight at midnight they'll be specks of dust. You'll live to see it all because you're a son of a whore with good bloodlines. Every conqueror has to preserve one specimen of the enemy he's vanquished so he can testify to the cataclysm to the generations to come. Preferably with all those superfluous details you need to restore a measure of credibility. That's why Nebuchadnezzar left Jeremiah alive. A very wise victor he was. Twenty-five hundred years after his death, you're all still weeping over that first temple he burned down. And that's why Titus, before burning the second temple, picked Joseph-Ben Matitiahou the traitor, gave him his dynastic name, Flavius, and made sure there was always ink in the inkwell, wine in the jug, food in the larder, and one or two cunts in his bed. So if one isn't weeping thanks to Jeremiah, one can still weep over the works of that son of a whore Flavius. And by the way, you must have noticed that both those guys were Cohens, and there are no worse sons of whores than the Cohanim. You look like a Cohen yourself. But what you don't know yet is how I'm going to screw both Nebuchadnezzar and Titus, due to my talent for thinking sideways and back. Just you wait. And by the way, please note that you too will have the use of a cunt. I have a feeling that you wouldn't feel so inspired without Liora's cunt.

Don't look at me like an idiot, it's annoying. I thought you'd understand. Don't you see? Whoever wants to stop what is happening today from happening today has to find a way to stop what happened yesterday from happening yesterday and what happened the day before from happening the day before. Only he who can stop today what happened the day before yesterday can also stop what will happen tomorrow because of what's happening today, if you see what I mean.

You look thirsty. Help yourself to some scotch. A war command center without scotch and caviar is like a whore without a cunt. I had one like that once, in Paris. She was from Brazil—but where were we? Right, about thinking sideways and back.

I'm sure you know about the wars of Halamish? General Halamish, remember, came up with the doctrine of warfare by spiral and got screwed by that doctrine because he fought his spiral war only in space, neglecting the dimension of time. Allow me to quote you a passage from the work of Amos Kenan, the great military theoretician—another son of a whore like you, by the way—to clarify matters.

The general pours both of us another glassful of scotch, then goes to a shelf and picks a thick volume, opens it to a marked page, and studies it for a few minutes. Then he closes the book, puts it on the table, and says, Let's not bore ourselves with the scribblings of that asshole. I'll summarize.

Before the time of Halamish, the army used the doctrine of the dead cow. Settlers would arrive and start a colony. One night the enemy would come and burn the fields. In the morning the settlers would find a dead cow in the fields. So they'd go to war. They'd conquer yet another tract of land, build another colony. The enemy would come at night. In the morning, another dead cow. Off to war again. That was the routine until General Halamish came along, God have mercy on his soul. He wasn't stupid, just an idiot. He invented the strategy of the one-eyed horse, also known as the strategy of the spiral. Halamish said that instead of charging straight ahead, the charge should go sideways, in a spiral. He came up with the famous war cry "Forward and around!"

When you charge sideways in a spiral, you hit the enemy from the east while he's waiting for you in the west. It's a great advantage. The trouble with a spiral is that it either converges toward its center or widens out to infinity. If you charge in an expanding spiral, you conquer the whole world. If you charge toward the center, you end up by charging right up your own ass. And when the spiral has a large diameter, it's hard to tell whether you're advancing from the beginning to the end or from the end to the beginning, and that's what happened to old Halamish. He moved in a spiral to take Tobruk, and only when the place went up in flames did he realize he had set fire to Tel Aviv with his own hands, so he put a bullet through his head.

The general puts the book back on the shelf, pours some more whiskey for both of us, and says, So that's Kenan's interpretation up to now, but he didn't quite figure out the essential point either. What's essential is that it's impossible to amend history after the fact. If you want to change the course of history, you don't do it by foreseeing the future but by screwing history in the ass, by means of the doctrine of retroaction. What most strategists fail to comprehend—and Halamish is a great example of the idiocy of all strategists after Hannibal—is that the doctrine of retroaction doesn't have to be applied only to space but can include time as well. We don't understand the concept of time correctly, we treat time as if it only extended in one direction, as if it proceeded from the point we call the beginning to the point we call the end. Bullshit. Time has no direction. Time is round and infinite, just as space is. And if you don't really enjoy still weeping twenty-five hundred years after Jeremiah, all you have to do is stop Nebuchadnezzar from burning the temple by means of the circumtemporal ballistic missile. I hope you're still with me here.

I say, Yes, I'm with you. But why Nineveh? I ask, pointing at the screen on the far right.

Ah, Nineveh, says the general. Because of Sennacherib. True, the plague laid waste his armies and he fled to Nineveh, but he had the gall to lay siege to Jerusalem, see Isaiah thirty-seven, verse thirty-six to the end: "And the angel of the Lord went forth, and smote in the camp of the Assyrians a hundred and fourscore and five thousand; and when the men arose early in the morning, behold, they were all dead corpses. So Sennacherib king of Assyria departed, and went, and returned, and dwelt at Nineveh." By the way, note the prophet's sense of humor. The corpses get up in the morning and see that they're all dead. But I say that isn't enough, that it is necessary to exterminate him totally even before he starts the siege of Jerusalem. Right now, he hasn't the faintest notion that at midnight tonight he and Nineveh and his entire army will be reduced to dust.

You're really serious about that, I say.

I certainly am. And after him there's Shalmaneser, because we can't overlook that business of the ten tribes, and I won't let him lay waste to Samaria. And by the way, since they both reigned in Nineveh, he'll inherit the missile of Sennacherib, so the two will be wiped out by the same missile.

I glance at the sentries. No way. As for the general himself, mission impossible. But it has to be done.

Am I right in assuming that the second screen on the right is aimed at Babylon?

Exactly. At midnight, Jerusalem time, Babylon will be blown away. Nebuchadnezzar will be blown away. And whoever's left, if anyone is, will have nothing to do but sit down and weep on the banks of the rivers of Babylon. You follow me?

I follow.

So then you know that it's Titus's turn after Neb. He's the third one on the right. Clearly, the only way to prevent the destruction of the temple is to strike Titus even before he sets out for Jerusalem.

Absolutely right.

Now, Titus, I'm going to get him in Spain. Because if I wait until he's already landed here with his armies, the whole country will be blown away too, see what I mean?

Sure do, I say. Great idea to catch him in Spain.

I don't have my Flavius in front of me right now, and I don't remember if Titus really did come from Spain when he moved against Eretz Israel, but that's no big deal. Where were we?

You see, the general goes on, if I wipe him out in Spain, as a consequence there will never be an Inquisition. There won't be a place for it to happen.

Nor will there be a Franco, I say, because he won't have a place to happen either.

Yeah, see, I was sure you'd understand. That's why I brought you here.

Two armed guards, one armed general, one girl, and me, with my bare hands. Even if I make the absolutely right decision about who I'll attack first, the others are going to react instantly. I have to create a situation in which no one has a chance to react from the very start.

I know that no one is going to believe me, but at this very moment Titus himself appears on the third screen from the right.

No mistake, it's him all right. I know him from his busts and statues. He is wearing purple and sky blue and sipping red wine from a goblet. There is a pretty woman beside him, maybe Berenice.

They're under surveillance twenty-four hours a day, says the general. We don't let them out of our sight for one minute. We listen to all their secrets. Yesterday we caught him announcing that he's going to arm a fleet and set sail for Jerusalem. That's why we picked tonight.

I have a question: Where is Khmelnitsky?

The general pushes a button. No Khmelnitsky appears on any of the screens.

He must be taking a shit, says the general. But he'll be back.

Titus pulls the sexy beauty closer and embraces her.

Look at that shithead, says the general. In a minute he's going to put out the light. I've been trying to catch him fucking for a week now, and he always puts out the lamps at the critical moment. Maybe there's a lesson there somewhere.

I'm holding my breath.

With a single motion Titus sweeps her silk robe to the floor.

She is dark-skinned, and the nipples on her breasts are huge. Her pubic hair isn't black, it's brown.

The general is a giant, all muscle. But even a giant who is all muscle has one spot where he can be mortally hit. The windpipe is not protected by any muscle.

Titus has taken off his tunic, he is naked. Berenice is on her knees, caressing the insides of his thighs.

I notice her large earring, shaped like a treble clef. Titus's phallus is beginning to rise.

Hey, you guys, the general roars. Come see what's going on here.

I bound up into the air to gain sufficient altitude and strike the general's windpipe in mid-leap with the edge of my hand.

Both guards manage to take a step forward while I kill him. The best marksman in the world can't be as accurate when he's moving as when he's standing still. I learned that once from Shaltiel, who had learned it in London at General Popsky's commando school.

Both guards fire simultaneously. But I'm back on the floor, the general's submachine gun in my hands, and I roll to the right. Even before I hit the ground, all the lights go out. No one has been paying attention to Liora. She must've been on her toes. Not only the lights but the screens and such go out all at once. She must have thrown the main switch.

Holding my breath, I start crawling.

Now everything is quiet. Total darkness, total silence. If one of them shoots, the flash will betray his position and he'll be dead. But when I shoot him, the flash from my weapon will show my position and I'll be dead. I can't fire even a single shot. But I have all the time in the world. As long as they haven't decided which one of them will sacrifice himself by shooting first or switching the lights back on, time is on my side entirely. Absolute darkness reigns, day and night, a darkness of three thousand years, three thousand dark-years.

Very slowly I take off a shoe. I'll throw it, but I have to make sure it doesn't hit a wall. It has to land on the floor to sound like someone stumbling in the dark.

I throw it and wait. For a second I'm afraid they'll react with intelligence, but then one of them fires. Had I been in that shoe, I would be dead. I fire slightly to the left of the flash and roll to my left. A right-handed person always rolls to the right. I hear the bullet go by on my right, and I fire again to the left of the second flash. I stay put.

He must be dead. There are no more shots. You're not so bad at murdering people yourself, the general had said, and we have read your dossier.

Now there are running footsteps in the dark. Kill me, soldier, Liora cries, kill me!

No one fires, no one kills. Then there's silence. No one running in the dark.

Light.

I get up, walk over to her. Come to Ein Harod, I say to her.

All three of them are dead, lying where they have fallen. Titus has made it into Berenice. I fire at the screen, I fire at all the screens.

We go back the way we came. We go up in the elevator, climb the ladder, raise the lid, and return to earth.

There's still the sentry at the gate. There is no moon, only the stars. I signal Liora to wait.

I crawl toward the gate. Very slowly. It isn't midnight yet, and I know that Nineveh and Babylon don't know it. I get close to the gate, see the guard. I take him out according to the manual.

What dossier, and what did they know about it? Goliath was a small-time murderer. David had more class.

We open the gate and hit the road.

She walks in front of me. Suddenly I want her more than I've ever wanted anything. Suddenly I am tired of it all, suddenly I don't give a damn, suddenly, well.

I no longer know if I'm murmuring and she's moaning or if I'm moaning and she's murmuring, just that I am now lying on my back gazing at the stars and she is by my side and my left arm is under her head and my right arm is holding her.

I want to die, she says. Help me die.

I hug her. Maybe I want to die too, but I can't.

I can't go on, she says. I don't want to. Help me die.

I hug her tighter. That is all I can do now, and all I can ask for.

Kill me now, please, she whispers, and falls asleep in my arms.

The report of a gun wakes me.

It is still before dawn. The general's submachine gun lies next to her, and she is dead.

I don't have a shovel, I can't dig a grave for her. I cover her body with stones.

I cry. I get up again and set out for Ein Harod. At the first light of dawn.

The valley of Jezreel lies before me. In all its splendor.

Here and there, groves of Tabor oak. Here and there, a verdant ravine. The whole valley is a blossoming meadow of green. Snowy almond trees, patches of anemones. All the first flowers of spring.

But there is nothing there.

I can't see anything.

No Balfouria, no Merhavia. No town of Afula. On the mountain across the valley, where lower Galilee begins, I can't see the slopes of Nazareth. Tel-Yosef isn't there, nor is Geva. No Road of the Rule, not a single eucalyptus tree, not a single water tower. What is this?

I walk down into the valley, into what once was the valley

of Jezreel. I walk straight ahead, guided by my senses, to the spring of Ein Harod.

The spring is there. I bend down and drink from its water. I look around.

Huge plane trees. Huge oleanders. Willows. The prairie. And trees I don't recognize. In the mud, tracks of wild pigs. I know those tracks well.

Some signs of panther. I know those too. And some other tracks I do not recognize. I head for the kibbutz of Ein Harod.

I get there. There is nothing. I recognize the spot, there's no mistake about it. I can find it in the dark, without a compass, without stars, without maps, without anything. Ein Harod is the place where everything starts, and I know how to get to the beginning. But there is nothing here.

I pull up a tuft of grass, breathe its scent. I am looking for signs but can't find any. Tracks left by a tractor. A crater left by a shell. Something to prove that there was something here once. But there is nothing.

Once I was taught what derelict foliage is: plants that testify that people have lived there. Perhaps there was a town here three thousand years ago. Even before there was a town, there may have been a village. Something. Somebody. Sometimes a village that's become a town then becomes a tumulus, and on this tumulus grow plants that testify that people once lived there. Mallow. Nettles. Fennel. Alder. And there's also thistle and thorn bushes and other varieties of derelict foliage, those that live off the minerals produced by the waste matter of people and their flocks, their cattle and domestic animals.

No. No mallow. No nettles. No fennel. No tumulus. None of that crumbly soil that once was ploughed and remains open, fertile, no longer virgin.

I don't know how long I have been standing here.

When I turn to look back, the world has gone dark.

I don't know if I'm blind. I no longer hear sounds, and I don't know if I am deaf.

I remember that pretty song I learned as a child: "How happy we are in Ein Harod."

Now, at last, I am happy. I am in Ein Harod.

# NOTES